ALL ALONE

(A Nicky Lyons FBI Suspense Thriller—Book Four)

BLAKE PIERCE

Blake Pierce

Blake Pierce is the USA Today bestselling author of the RILEY PAGE mystery series, which includes seventeen books. Blake Pierce is also the author of the MACKENZIE WHITE mystery series, comprising fourteen books; of the AVERY BLACK mystery series, comprising six books; of the KERI LOCKE mystery series, comprising five books; of the MAKING OF RILEY PAIGE mystery series, comprising six books; of the KATE WISE mystery series, comprising seven books; of the CHLOE FINE psychological suspense mystery, comprising six books; of the JESSIE HUNT psychological suspense thriller series, comprising twenty six books; of the AU PAIR psychological suspense thriller series, comprising three books; of the ZOE PRIME mystery series, comprising six books; of the ADELE SHARP mystery series, comprising sixteen books, of the EUROPEAN VOYAGE cozy mystery series, comprising six books; of the LAURA FROST FBI suspense thriller, comprising eleven books; of the ELLA DARK FBI suspense thriller, comprising fourteen books (and counting); of the A YEAR IN EUROPE cozy mystery series, comprising nine books, of the AVA GOLD mystery series, comprising six books; of the RACHEL GIFT mystery series, comprising ten books (and counting); of the VALERIE LAW mystery series, comprising nine books (and counting); of the PAIGE KING mystery series, comprising eight books (and counting); of the MAY MOORE mystery series, comprising eleven books (and counting); the CORA SHIELDS mystery series, comprising five books (and counting); of the NICKY LYONS mystery series, comprising seven books (and counting), of the CAMI LARK mystery series, comprising five books (and counting), of the AMBER YOUNG mystery series, comprising five books (and counting), and of the new DAISY FORTUNE mystery series, comprising five books (and counting).

An avid reader and lifelong fan of the mystery and thriller genres, Blake loves to hear from you, so please feel free to visit www.blakepierceauthor.com to learn more and stay in touch.

ISBN: 978-1-0943-8055-1

BOOKS BY BLAKE PIERCE

DAISY FORTUNE MYSTERY SERIES
NEED YOU (Book #1)
CLAIM YOU (Book #2)
CRAVE YOU (Book #3)
CHOOSE YOU (Book #4)
CHASE YOU (Book #5)

AMBER YOUNG MYSTERY SERIES
ABSENT PITY (Book #1)
ABSENT REMORSE (Book #2)
ABSENT FEELING (Book #3)
ABSENT MERCY (Book #4)
ABSENT REASON (Book #5)

CAMI LARK MYSTERY SERIES
JUST ME (Book #1)
JUST OUTSIDE (Book #2)
JUST RIGHT (Book #3)
JUST FORGET (Book #4)
JUST ONCE (Book #5)

NICKY LYONS MYSTERY SERIES
ALL MINE (Book #1)
ALL HIS (Book #2)
ALL HE SEES (Book #3)
ALL ALONE (Book #4)
ALL FOR ONE (Book #5)
ALL HE TAKES (Book #6)
ALL FOR ME (Book #7)

CORA SHIELDS MYSTERY SERIES
UNDONE (Book #1)
UNWANTED (Book #2)
UNHINGED (Book #3)
UNSAID (Book #4)
UNGLUED (Book #5)

MAY MOORE SUSPENSE THRILLER
NEVER RUN (Book #1)
NEVER TELL (Book #2)
NEVER LIVE (Book #3)
NEVER HIDE (Book #4)
NEVER FORGIVE (Book #5)
NEVER AGAIN (Book #6)
NEVER LOOK BACK (Book #7)
NEVER FORGET (Book #8)
NEVER LET GO (Book #9)
NEVER PRETEND (Book #10)
NEVER HESITATE (Book #11)

PAIGE KING MYSTERY SERIES
THE GIRL HE PINED (Book #1)
THE GIRL HE CHOSE (Book #2)
THE GIRL HE TOOK (Book #3)
THE GIRL HE WISHED (Book #4)
THE GIRL HE CROWNED (Book #5)
THE GIRL HE WATCHED (Book #6)
THE GIRL HE WANTED (Book #7)
THE GIRL HE CLAIMED (Book #8)

VALERIE LAW MYSTERY SERIES
NO MERCY (Book #1)
NO PITY (Book #2)
NO FEAR (Book #3)
NO SLEEP (Book #4)
NO QUARTER (Book #5)
NO CHANCE (Book #6)
NO REFUGE (Book #7)
NO GRACE (Book #8)
NO ESCAPE (Book #9)

RACHEL GIFT MYSTERY SERIES
HER LAST WISH (Book #1)
HER LAST CHANCE (Book #2)
HER LAST HOPE (Book #3)
HER LAST FEAR (Book #4)
HER LAST CHOICE (Book #5)
HER LAST BREATH (Book #6)

HER LAST MISTAKE (Book #7)
HER LAST DESIRE (Book #8)
HER LAST REGRET (Book #9)
HER LAST HOUR (Book #10)

AVA GOLD MYSTERY SERIES
CITY OF PREY (Book #1)
CITY OF FEAR (Book #2)
CITY OF BONES (Book #3)
CITY OF GHOSTS (Book #4)
CITY OF DEATH (Book #5)
CITY OF VICE (Book #6)

A YEAR IN EUROPE
A MURDER IN PARIS (Book #1)
DEATH IN FLORENCE (Book #2)
VENGEANCE IN VIENNA (Book #3)
A FATALITY IN SPAIN (Book #4)

ELLA DARK FBI SUSPENSE THRILLER
GIRL, ALONE (Book #1)
GIRL, TAKEN (Book #2)
GIRL, HUNTED (Book #3)
GIRL, SILENCED (Book #4)
GIRL, VANISHED (Book 5)
GIRL ERASED (Book #6)
GIRL, FORSAKEN (Book #7)
GIRL, TRAPPED (Book #8)
GIRL, EXPENDABLE (Book #9)
GIRL, ESCAPED (Book #10)
GIRL, HIS (Book #11)
GIRL, LURED (Book #12)
GIRL, MISSING (Book #13)
GIRL, UNKNOWN (Book #14)

LAURA FROST FBI SUSPENSE THRILLER
ALREADY GONE (Book #1)
ALREADY SEEN (Book #2)
ALREADY TRAPPED (Book #3)
ALREADY MISSING (Book #4)
ALREADY DEAD (Book #5)

ALREADY TAKEN (Book #6)
ALREADY CHOSEN (Book #7)
ALREADY LOST (Book #8)
ALREADY HIS (Book #9)
ALREADY LURED (Book #10)
ALREADY COLD (Book #11)

EUROPEAN VOYAGE COZY MYSTERY SERIES
MURDER (AND BAKLAVA) (Book #1)
DEATH (AND APPLE STRUDEL) (Book #2)
CRIME (AND LAGER) (Book #3)
MISFORTUNE (AND GOUDA) (Book #4)
CALAMITY (AND A DANISH) (Book #5)
MAYHEM (AND HERRING) (Book #6)

ADELE SHARP MYSTERY SERIES
LEFT TO DIE (Book #1)
LEFT TO RUN (Book #2)
LEFT TO HIDE (Book #3)
LEFT TO KILL (Book #4)
LEFT TO MURDER (Book #5)
LEFT TO ENVY (Book #6)
LEFT TO LAPSE (Book #7)
LEFT TO VANISH (Book #8)
LEFT TO HUNT (Book #9)
LEFT TO FEAR (Book #10)
LEFT TO PREY (Book #11)
LEFT TO LURE (Book #12)
LEFT TO CRAVE (Book #13)
LEFT TO LOATHE (Book #14)
LEFT TO HARM (Book #15)
LEFT TO RUIN (Book #16)

THE AU PAIR SERIES
ALMOST GONE (Book#1)
ALMOST LOST (Book #2)
ALMOST DEAD (Book #3)

ZOE PRIME MYSTERY SERIES
FACE OF DEATH (Book#1)
FACE OF MURDER (Book #2)

FACE OF FEAR (Book #3)
FACE OF MADNESS (Book #4)
FACE OF FURY (Book #5)
FACE OF DARKNESS (Book #6)

A JESSIE HUNT PSYCHOLOGICAL SUSPENSE SERIES
THE PERFECT WIFE (Book #1)
THE PERFECT BLOCK (Book #2)
THE PERFECT HOUSE (Book #3)
THE PERFECT SMILE (Book #4)
THE PERFECT LIE (Book #5)
THE PERFECT LOOK (Book #6)
THE PERFECT AFFAIR (Book #7)
THE PERFECT ALIBI (Book #8)
THE PERFECT NEIGHBOR (Book #9)
THE PERFECT DISGUISE (Book #10)
THE PERFECT SECRET (Book #11)
THE PERFECT FAÇADE (Book #12)
THE PERFECT IMPRESSION (Book #13)
THE PERFECT DECEIT (Book #14)
THE PERFECT MISTRESS (Book #15)
THE PERFECT IMAGE (Book #16)
THE PERFECT VEIL (Book #17)
THE PERFECT INDISCRETION (Book #18)
THE PERFECT RUMOR (Book #19)
THE PERFECT COUPLE (Book #20)
THE PERFECT MURDER (Book #21)
THE PERFECT HUSBAND (Book #22)
THE PERFECT SCANDAL (Book #23)
THE PERFECT MASK (Book #24)
THE PERFECT RUSE (Book #25)
THE PERFECT VENEER (Book #26)

CHLOE FINE PSYCHOLOGICAL SUSPENSE SERIES
NEXT DOOR (Book #1)
A NEIGHBOR'S LIE (Book #2)
CUL DE SAC (Book #3)
SILENT NEIGHBOR (Book #4)
HOMECOMING (Book #5)
TINTED WINDOWS (Book #6)

KATE WISE MYSTERY SERIES

IF SHE KNEW (Book #1)
IF SHE SAW (Book #2)
IF SHE RAN (Book #3)
IF SHE HID (Book #4)
IF SHE FLED (Book #5)
IF SHE FEARED (Book #6)
IF SHE HEARD (Book #7)

THE MAKING OF RILEY PAIGE SERIES

WATCHING (Book #1)
WAITING (Book #2)
LURING (Book #3)
TAKING (Book #4)
STALKING (Book #5)
KILLING (Book #6)

RILEY PAIGE MYSTERY SERIES

ONCE GONE (Book #1)
ONCE TAKEN (Book #2)
ONCE CRAVED (Book #3)
ONCE LURED (Book #4)
ONCE HUNTED (Book #5)
ONCE PINED (Book #6)
ONCE FORSAKEN (Book #7)
ONCE COLD (Book #8)
ONCE STALKED (Book #9)
ONCE LOST (Book #10)
ONCE BURIED (Book #11)
ONCE BOUND (Book #12)
ONCE TRAPPED (Book #13)
ONCE DORMANT (Book #14)
ONCE SHUNNED (Book #15)
ONCE MISSED (Book #16)
ONCE CHOSEN (Book #17)

MACKENZIE WHITE MYSTERY SERIES

BEFORE HE KILLS (Book #1)
BEFORE HE SEES (Book #2)
BEFORE HE COVETS (Book #3)
BEFORE HE TAKES (Book #4)

BEFORE HE NEEDS (Book #5)
BEFORE HE FEELS (Book #6)
BEFORE HE SINS (Book #7)
BEFORE HE HUNTS (Book #8)
BEFORE HE PREYS (Book #9)
BEFORE HE LONGS (Book #10)
BEFORE HE LAPSES (Book #11)
BEFORE HE ENVIES (Book #12)
BEFORE HE STALKS (Book #13)
BEFORE HE HARMS (Book #14)

AVERY BLACK MYSTERY SERIES
CAUSE TO KILL (Book #1)
CAUSE TO RUN (Book #2)
CAUSE TO HIDE (Book #3)
CAUSE TO FEAR (Book #4)
CAUSE TO SAVE (Book #5)
CAUSE TO DREAD (Book #6)

KERI LOCKE MYSTERY SERIES
A TRACE OF DEATH (Book #1)
A TRACE OF MURDER (Book #2)
A TRACE OF VICE (Book #3)
A TRACE OF CRIME (Book #4)
A TRACE OF HOPE (Book #5)

PROLOGUE

Natalia stretched her legs out on her outdoor chaise, feeling the sun's warmth on her sun-kissed skin. This was the life. Her own private beach, no one here to bother her unless she wanted them to. She adjusted her sunglasses and peered out at the ocean spread out before her, crystal blue in the afternoon sun.

She couldn't help but steal a glance at her phone on the table beside her. Still no texts.

Natalia sighed, anxious and eager to hear back, but she might have to wait a while longer. Until then, she stretched again and basked in the sun.

"I thought you might enjoy a cocktail," a voice said from behind her.

Her head snapped up and she smiled when she saw the person walking toward her. He was tall, at least six-three, and muscular. She was certain he worked out. He had a very nice body with a broad chest and flat stomach. He had on a pair of khaki shorts and a polo shirt, the sleeves of which were pushed up to his elbows, exposing his forearms. His skin was a beautiful bronze color as if he spent a lot of time in the sun. Enrique offered her the cocktail, and Natalia smiled, grateful.

"Thank you, Enrique," she said.

"Did you need a refill on your fruit, miss?" he asked, nodding toward the empty dish of fruit beside her. Natalia ate a strict raw food diet—this figure of hers didn't come without work.

"No, but thank you for asking."

"Very well. If you need anything, please let me know," he said.

"Thanks, I will."

He went to leave, but Natalia found herself not wanting to be alone.

"Enrique, where are you from?" she asked. Natalia liked to know a little about the people who worked for her family.

"I was born in Mexico, but my family moved to the United States when I was very young. I have lived here ever since," he said.

"What brought you to work for my father?"

"I met Mr. Cavazos a few years ago. I was working for a friend, a poor man. Mr. Cavazos said he could help me, so he hired me to drive him. He said that I would learn so much by the time I was done and would be able to find work wherever I wanted. He was right. I was working for him a few weeks later. I have never worked for anyone as generous or kind as he is," he said.

"He...he's very generous," Natalia agreed. She didn't want Enrique talking to her about her father or the family. She was sure he would say something she would regret.

"He is a good boss, also. I have worked for him for ten years, and I have never been in trouble," he said with a wink.

Natalia couldn't help but smile. Enrique was charming her. At the same time, she could see the way his body leaned back toward the path that would lead to the vacation house, so he probably had more work to do. Natalia didn't mind his company, but she let him go.

"Thank you, Enrique," she said.

"It was my pleasure," he said.

Natalia watched him walk away, admiring the way his body moved. She glanced at her phone again. Still nothing.

Natalia sat in her chaise, enjoying the sun and the breeze. She felt certain that Enrique had gone for lunch or for the day. She was alone, and she was okay with it. She enjoyed being by herself.

She picked up her book and started to read, but soon she heard a sound off in the distance.

It was like a motor.

What the hell? This beach was private; no boats were supposed to pass it. But she lifted her sunglasses to look out at the sea. Sure enough, a motorboat was coming toward the beach, getting closer.

Annoyed, Natalia stood up. Maybe the boat didn't realize where it was going. She waved her arms in the air and yelled, "Hey, get out of here! Private beach!"

The boat kept coming. Natalia didn't like this. What if the driver was drunk? It was probably an accident waiting to happen. A figure appeared on the boat as it got closer, and she squinted, trying to see who it was, but she couldn't tell.

A bad feeling churned inside her.

Natalia tried to keep her distance, but she didn't want the boat to hit her beach. She started to run toward the water yelling at the driver, "Hey! Watch it! You're going to hit my beach!" She felt the wind whip up, blowing her long, black hair into her face.

The boat didn't stop. As it got closer, Natalia could see the figure on the boat was swaying. The boat kept coming toward the beach, but it wasn't speeding—the pace was steady, and she realized that if it did come into shore, it would get caught in the sand first before crashing.

Just as Natalia was about to grab her phone and call for help, the figure toppled over and fell straight into the water.

Natalia yelped, alarmed. Something was wrong. The person on this boat—they were hurt.

She had to help them.

She ran into the water until she was ankle-deep. She heard calling from the boat, but she didn't know what the person was saying.

"Hey, are you okay?" she yelled.

The boat was coming closer to shore. It slowed down, but it hadn't stopped.

"Hello?" she yelled again. She frantically looked for any sign of the person in the water, but she couldn't see them.

At that moment, something splashed.

Something behind her.

Natalia whipped around—just as something hard smacked into the back of her skull.

Her body went weak, falling into the cold water below.

All at once, the world faded.

CHAPTER ONE

Sitting in the parking lot outside of the prison, Agent Nicky Lyons of the FBI took a breath as she anticipated the voice on the other end of the line. Her father's voice. Her father, who she hadn't spoken to in years.

"Hi, Dad," she'd said only moments ago, and now, she waited.

But he didn't talk back.

Holding her breath, Nicky gazed out at the prison that stood before her: a giant, impenetrable fortress in the afternoon sun. It was Felix Anderson—a man she'd taken down two cases ago—who had convinced her to call her father, after all these years.

The truth was, Nicky had let Felix get into her head. Felix himself had been a kidnapper before Nicky had apprehended him, obsessed specifically with sisters—and that had struck a chord for Nicky.

Nicky and her own sister, Rosie, had been kidnapped themselves as teenagers. Nicky got away. Rosie didn't. And Felix, somehow, knew about their case.

Nicky had been damn convinced he knew something about the kidnapper too. But all he'd told her was to talk to her father.

Truthfully, Nicky didn't know why she'd listened. She was desperate. Her boss, Chief Eric Franco, had said the FBI could officially re-open the case of Rosie Lyons if Nicky could come up with some tangible evidence that Rosie was even still out there—or that Felix Anderson actually knew something.

But her father? Nicky knew it was ridiculous. Her dad was a drunk before Rosie went missing and he was a drunk after. They had a bad relationship before, and now they had no relationship at all.

So, Nicky wasn't surprised that she was still waiting for her dad's voice to come through on the other end of the line.

Last time she'd checked, he didn't like her as much as she didn't like him.

And how is she supposed to claim that he is her best chance at finding evidence about Rosie?

"Dad?" Nicky tried again, and still, there was silence.

She almost hung up the phone, she really did. But then, finally, she heard him speak.

"I'm...Nicky? Is that really you?"

Nicky's mouth nearly dropped at the familiar voice. It was so strange to talk to him again. For once, he didn't sound completely wasted, but she couldn't be sure yet.

"Yes," she said. "It's me."

"Wow..." he said. "It's been a long time."

"I know," Nicky said.

Silence. While they weren't face-to-face—he was back in Nelly, West Virginia while she was in Florida—Nicky could feel the tension and the awkwardness.

There would be no apologies here. Her father and her were never good at that.

"What do you need?" he finally said.

At least he wasn't being that rude, but there was still nothing warm about his tone.

"Listen," she said. "I know this is weird. I'm not sure why I'm bothering you at all, honestly." She paused. "I just need your help."

"And what could I possibly help you with?" he asked.

Nicky took a breath. If she and her father ever had one thing they could never agree on, it was how to talk about Rosie. He wasn't going to take this well, but Nicky had to push on.

"It's about Rosie. She's been missing for so long, but...I'm still looking."

His silence was significant. Those two words—Rosie and missing—had an effect on him, whether he wanted to admit it or not.

"Listen, I'm not looking for you to be like...an ear for me," Nicky said, biting her tongue as she spoke. "I'm not looking for any kind of reconciliation here. I just...I just want to know if you can help me. If you can help Rosie."

"Nicky." Her father's voice was firm. "You know I don't know anything about what happened to your sister. The only person who really knows is you."

Nicky bit back her reply as anger and frustration flared up inside her. Her father had always blamed her, and Nicky had always blamed herself too.

It struck a chord.

But Nicky didn't know what happened to Rosie. She didn't know who the kidnapper was, even if she was one of his victims too. Nicky was still haunted by the memories of how she and Rosie were taken by that man and kept in that cabin, all those years ago. She was still shaken by the memory of her and Rosie escaping, only for Rosie to fall behind. Nicky got away. Rosie didn't.

She was never seen again.

And now, Nicky still knew nothing about the man who had taken them.

But Nicky couldn't keep this on herself. This wasn't about her, and it wasn't about her relationship with her father either. He could say what he wanted. It was Felix Anderson who brought them together, and maybe he was the key to all of it.

"Dad," Nicky said. "Do you know a man named Felix Anderson?"

She paused. "He was in prison. He's a kidnapper. And he told me to talk to you to find Rosie."

Nicky could hear her father's voice falter over the phone.

"Felix Anderson," he repeated. "It doesn't sound familiar. What's he got to do with your sister? I don't get why you're calling me out of the blue like this. If this is a joke, or you're trying to piss me off, then it's working."

Nicky's teeth clenched. And here it was: her father's true colors.

Bastard. He'd never taken responsibility for anything in this life.

"I'm not," she said. "I'm not trying to piss you off, Dad. I'm trying to find my sister. I just needed to talk to you."

"You're not trying to find her," her father said. "You were already with her, and you let her go."

For a moment, she couldn't reply. But she pushed back the feelings of anger and bitterness toward her father. She had to be strong now. She couldn't let emotions get in the way.

"Yes, I am," Nicky said. "This Felix Anderson guy said I need to talk to you."

"Felix Anderson," her father echoed. "He sounds like a piece of shit, and you're telling me that you're listening to him?"

Nicky almost lost it. *Don't you dare talk to me like this.*

"I've already told you," she said, her voice hard. "I don't want to get you involved, but if there's any chance you know something or you heard anything—"

"There's no way I can help you with this," her father had replied with finality. "Look for your sister yourself."

And then he'd hung up.

Nicky told herself she couldn't be surprised. This was her father: cold, angry, and rude.

Despite that, she was left with a surge of emotion.

Her sister. Felix Anderson.

She had no idea what to do.

But she knew one thing.

She had to keep searching.

As Nicky sat in the parking lot of the prison, she realized that her father was right: she had to find her sister herself. Her dad wasn't going to help her and talking to him did nothing but stir up old feelings of anger and betrayal.

She was on her own, and she was going to be searching for Rosie until the day she died.

She just didn't know how to go about it. Why did Felix say to call her dad?

Was her dad lying?

Was Felix trying to frame him?

Or maybe it was someone else, someone Felix had talked to in the past?

Still, she couldn't help but ask herself—and her father—if she had done nothing wrong. If she had let Rosie go.

Maybe it was all her fault.

She was the one who had left Rosie behind at that lake house all those years ago.

Remembering that stung her more than she'd ever admit to anyone.

But she had to face reality: Rosie was gone, and Nicky was here. She became an FBI agent to save other girls like Rosie. But even after all this time, Nicky wanted nothing more than to save Rosie. This was the closest she'd ever come to an answer, and yet she still had nothing.

Tears burned Nicky's eyes, but she blinked them away.

She was alone, but she couldn't afford to let herself be defeated.

In truth, she didn't want to fail.

There was too much riding on the line.

It was time to start somewhere else.

She had to do something else to find her sister.

She had to do something else to find the kidnapper.

But what? She was at a dead end. She didn't know what to do—all she knew was that she wasn't about to talk to Felix again, not right now. She started her car and pulled out of the parking lot. She didn't even know where she was going.

She just had to go.

As Nicky merged onto the highway, the phone call she just had with her dad settled in. She'd really talked to him. And while it hadn't been nuclear, it hadn't been good either. What was she supposed to do now? As she gripped the steering wheel and made her way into highway traffic headed back toward Jacksonville, Nicky was surprised to feel her eyes stinging.

No, she thought. *No, I won't cry. I won't...*

But it was too late. She didn't want to cry, but she couldn't help it. Her mind flashed over her father's words and tone to her...and she thought back to that night. That night she left Rosie, alone in the woods with the kidnapper. The night she selfishly escaped.

The night that changed everything.

If Nicky had stayed with Rosie, maybe they could have found a way out together. She should have gone back. Felix was right before—Nicky had been weak to leave her sister behind.

So weak.

She couldn't help it. She pulled onto the shoulder of the highway and stopped the car, then leaned over and buried her face in her arms.

She couldn't stop the tears.

There was so much she wanted to say to her dad, so many things they could've talked about. Instead, they had gone at each other like they always did. It was too late. It had always been too late, and they'd never found a way to take the first step, to be better.

Nicky cried until she had no tears left. When she looked back up, she felt a little lighter, a little calmer. She let herself breathe for a moment, let her heart slow down. And then she took a deep breath, wiped her face with her hands, and thought about what she was going to do.

If she couldn't do it by talking to her father, then she had to do it another way.

Just as Nicky was collecting herself and telling herself to get it back together, her phone vibrated. She took it out and saw Chief Franco's name across her screen. In a way, it relieved her. She'd been given the day off, but maybe they had more work. More work would be good. It would stop her from thinking so much.

"Chief?" Nicky said into the phone.

"Lyons." Chief Franco sounded frantic and winded. She'd seen him only a few hours ago—what was this about?

"What's going on?" she asked, her breath catching.

"I know I gave you the day off, but—"

"Don't worry about that," Nicky said. "What happened?"

"Another girl has been kidnapped," the chief said. "Lyons. You need to get to the scene of the crime now. I'm sending you the details."

With that, the call ended, and Nicky stared at her phone, waiting for her next orders.

She had never heard the chief so urgent before. Whatever this case was, it had to be huge.

CHAPTER TWO

Nicky hurried to a lavish five-star resort on a private beach in Southern Florida. It stood on a plot of land surrounded by a towering fence. The fence was hidden by overgrown palm trees but not nearly enough for it to be invisible. The door looked like solid gold and the windows were all glass, immaculate and flawless. A private beach bordered on one side, and the other was dotted with tropical palms and overgrown wildflowers. There were private boats in the water and a speedboat docked near the shore, but Nicky just needed to get inside.

She pulled open the doors with a firm press of her palm and entered the lobby, but two men wearing suits with sunglasses stopped her.

"Ma'am, this resort is closed," Nicky said.

What the hell? If Nicky didn't know any better, she'd think these guys were secret service. They definitely didn't look like hotel security—even for a five-star resort.

She flashed her badge and gave them a stern look. "I'm Agent Lyons with the FBI. I was called here."

The two men in sunglasses looked at each other, then at their watches. "Well, you're late."

Nicky glared at them, but when she didn't make a move, the men nodded.

"Come on."

The two men led Nicky through the hotel, taking her toward the back entrance, where it opened up to a patio that led down to the private beach. They stepped outside and into the warm late-afternoon sun.

Nicky couldn't help but glare at her *escorts.* "You two don't seem like hotel security," she commented.

"Secret service," one man said without looking back. "It's right this way."

So, they were secret service. Nicky's alarm bells were going off.

"Why would secret service agents be here?" she asked. "This place doesn't seem like it needs protection."

"Just follow," the other guard said nonchalantly.

She didn't like how this resort was being protected, with secret service guarding the place. It was strange. But she needed to get to the bottom of this. That was her job. So, she followed them to the beach, where a group of cops and other crime scene investigators were already at work. Not to mention, there was so much security and so many secret service agents that it was making Nicky's head spin.

Nicky slipped into the crowd behind the agents, staying out of the way. She watched as they examined the sand, the water, and the private speedboat. She watched as they combed the grounds and looked around the hotel. Her head was spinning, and she had no idea what was going on.

"Where's Chief Franco?" she asked the agents.

They said nothing. Annoyed, Nicky focused on moving through the crowd.

And that was when she saw him.

Chief Franco, standing face-to-face with an older man. Caucasian. Thinning white hair. Wearing a suit.

Nicky's stomach fell so far to the floor, she nearly tripped over it.

Standing in front of her was the vice president of the United States.

Vice President Steven Cavazos, honored war veteran and right-hand to the president.

Nicky thought she was imagining things. That it was a stunt double or an impersonator.

But no, this was him. She stopped in her tracks but checked herself when the two secret service agents looked back at her.

She didn't want to make a scene.

But she couldn't believe it. Why would Steven Cavazos be here? Why would the vice president be at a kidnapping crime scene?

She stayed back as far as she could, watching the conversation between the two men. It was tense. The chief—normally so confident and calm—looked like a deer in headlights.

The vice president of the United States in his face.

Nicky crossed her fingers, hoping that whatever the chief said would be enough to calm him down.

Please, she thought. *Don't let him blow it.*

But the chief himself was nearly spitting as he turned to face her.

"Agent Lyons," Chief Franco said, his voice low and hushed. "Do you have a moment?"

Nicky swallowed but nodded. Her eyes locked on the vice president's, and she found herself at a loss for words.

"Mr. Vice President," Franco said, turning to Steven, "this is Agent Nicky Lyons."

Shaking, Nicky held a firm hand out. Steven Cavazos was more than a politician—in the public's eye, he was the perfect image of a family man. Everyone knew that he loved his wife and his daughter, Natalia, and Nicky respected that aspect of him. She wished she had worn something other than cargo shorts and a tank top. She wished she had worn a tie and taken her hair down. But she had dressed down for the day off, and now she was paying for it dearly.

Nicky wanted to take it back. She wanted to run. She couldn't believe she was doing this.

Steven Cavazos took her hand, and she nearly fainted at his touch.

"Agent Lyons," he said, his voice a familiar drawl. "Thank you for coming."

The way he said it—the way he looked at her—Nicky felt like she was going to pass out.

"It's my pleasure," she said. "It's an honor to meet you, Mr. Vice President."

"Steven is fine," he said.

"Sir, I couldn't," she said, the warmth of his hand still on hers.

"Please." He smiled, though his eyes were crestfallen. "I insist."

Nicky found herself smiling despite herself. But she tried to hide it with a small cough and snapped herself back to the present.

Clearly, something serious had happened here. She focused on Chief Franco, just as somebody else broke through the crowd.

Nicky's heart nearly stopped. It was Agent Ken Walker, her partner. In all the chaos, she'd barely taken a moment to think about him—or about the moment they'd recently shared together. Nicky and Ken had grown closer on their last case together, and Nicky even felt a strange moment of attraction toward him. But she pushed that aside as he hurried over to them, stopping in his tracks when he saw the vice president. Clearly, Ken hadn't been fully informed of what the hell was going on either.

"Sir," he said, extending a hand to Steven. "Mr. Vice President, it's an honor to meet you."

Steven shook it firmly. "You must be Agent Walker. Chief Franco told me about you."

Ken looked at Nicky, then at Franco. "Sir?" he said, his voice still hushed.

Franco nodded toward the beach. "Come with me," he said. "All three of you."

Nicky fell into step behind Ken as they headed toward the beach. He was the only one that seemed calm and collected, but she knew him well enough by now to see the subtle signs on his face that showed he was also thrown a bit off-guard. She wondered if he had any idea what was going on here.

They gathered in front of the water. When Franco turned to face them this time, his face was serious. Serious and completely cold.

Cold as steel.

"I don't know where to start," Franco said. "So, I think I'll just start with the basics."

Nicky's curiosity was killing her, but she stayed quiet, knowing better than to speak up. Steven stood, quietly and stoically, beside them, and Nicky took note of the several secret service agents who were watching his back the whole time, standing around the beach.

Chief Franco sighed. "I'm sorry to say, but the vice president's daughter—Natalia Cavazos—has gone missing. She's been gone for at least four hours now."

He paused. The sound of the waves filled the air.

"And?" Ken said, raising an eyebrow.

"And," Franco continued, "there are signs that point to her being taken against her will. There are signs that point to a kidnapping."

Nicky's eyes went wide.

"This is a serious matter, Agent Walker," Franco said.

Nicky felt like she was going to be sick.

Ken just shook his head, his voice incredulous. "How can you be so sure?"

"Because," Steven cut in, "my daughter would never leave her cell phone behind. She's a twenty-year-old girl, and one of my most trusted workers saw her on the beach. Then, she vanished into thin air. I had two agents who were supposed to be watching her, and—" He took a breath, anger growing on his face.

Nicky would not want to be the agents who lost the vice president's daughter.

"It's a kidnapping." Franco narrowed his eyes. "I don't typically like to react on a gut feeling, but a gut feeling is all we have."

"I can't believe it," Ken said.

Nicky agreed. She almost couldn't believe it herself.

"What do you need from us?" Ken said.

“I need you to find my daughter,” Steven said. “I need you to do whatever it takes to bring her back home. Chief Franco tells me you two are exemplary. Agent Lyons, I heard you were the one who found Senator Gregory’s daughter.”

Nicky saw him look at her, and she wished she could sink into a hole. She *had* been the one to find Masie Gregory. Unfortunately, Masie was not found alive.

“Sir,” she said. “We’ll do everything we can.”

“Agreed,” Ken said. “We’ll find her, Sir. I guarantee it.”

It was a lot to promise to a very important person, and it veered away from Nicky’s main goal—which was to find the girls on the top ten list Senator Gregory had given her. That was the entire point of the task force Nicky had been put in charge of, with Ken Walker and their tech, Grace Taylor. But if this was where Chief Franco wanted them—where the vice president wanted them—then Nicky would have to push forward.

Still, this felt like more pressure than ever before. This was the vice president’s daughter.

If they found her, they’d be heroes.

But if they didn’t...

Nicky could think of no worse way to fail than by letting the vice president’s daughter—and probably his only child—wind up dead somewhere.

Suddenly, two agents—a tall, lean man and a short, slim woman—hurried over to the vice president. Like the others in the secret service, they were far from inconspicuous, wearing black suits and sunglasses. Nicky frowned as they hurried over, and the vice president shot them a scornful look.

“You two—get out of my sight, now.”

Damn, Nicky thought. If the VP ever talked to her that way, she would probably die of humiliation and disgrace. She could only assume these were the two agents who were in charge of Natalia when she went missing.

“Sir, with all due respect—” the man started.

“Get out of my sight,” Steven said. “Now. I’m handing this off to the FBI.”

“But—”

“I said now!” Steven bellowed.

The two agents ran off. Nicky watched as they scurried away, and she found herself wishing she could have been the one who was in charge of Natalie before she went missing. Then, she'd never have gone missing at all. She felt herself grinding her teeth and hoped no one would notice. She didn't have much experience with the secret service, but she needed to talk to those two and find out what the hell happened. Had they just been reckless and careless? Or did something truly sinister happen to Natalia, and they could not stop it?

She looked at Ken. As usual, he was the one person who understood her. She ignored the tingling feeling in her chest as they looked at Chief Franco and the vice president. The vice president...he was one of the most important people in the world. Nicky could only imagine what would happen if she and Ken somehow let the vice president down. It would be the biggest failure of her life.

The enormity of the situation was dawning on her, more and more with each passing second.

"I'm leaving this in your capable hands," the VP said. He turned to walk away, and two other secret service agents followed suit, closely mirroring him. As he disappeared back toward the resort, Nicky was still in awe—partially starstruck but mostly baffled. But she had to focus. Natalia Cavazos was now the top priority, and Nicky had to treat this like every other job.

"Chief, we need to be filled in," Nicky said. "Fill us in on everything."

Chief Franco nodded. "The girl's phone was found over there, by that chaise lounge." He pointed to a setup with a chaise and a table under an umbrella. "Forensics already swept it. We've got nothing concrete. Nothing that tells us what happened to her or where she went."

"I have an idea," Ken said. "What if she went down to the beach?"

"That's what I thought too," Franco said. "But my people searched the beach, and they found nothing."

"Maybe she went out in the water?" Nicky questioned.

"Natalia wasn't a swimmer, according to her father," said the chief. "She just suntanned. It would be out of character for her to go swimming."

"Right." Nicky looked down the beach, catching sight of the two secret service agents who the VP had been reeming out. She looked at Ken, and he nodded.

They were who they needed to speak to first about this. Losing the president's daughter was not a small feat. They had some answering to do.

CHAPTER THREE

Nicky and Ken made their way over to the agents. Nicky saw from the expressions on their faces that they knew they were in deep shit. One of them, the woman, was staring at the ground. The man had his hands in his pockets. Neither one of them would look at Nicky and Ken when they got close.

"What the hell happened?" Ken said.

"We...we don't know," the woman said. Nicky could see tears in her eyes. She turned to her partner, the tall, lean man.

"We tried our best to watch her," he said. "She just...vanished. We only left for maybe five minutes."

Nicky's eyes went wide. "What do you mean you didn't see anything? You left her alone?"

The two agents looked at each other, then sighed.

"You don't understand," said the man. "Natalia ordered us to keep our distance from her. She's very adamant on her privacy."

"And you listened to her?" Nicky said. "You just let her disappear?"

The man looked down at Nicky sternly. "You have no idea what she's like."

"That's bullshit," Nicky said. "She's the vice president's daughter, not a goddamned celebrity."

The woman's eyebrows went up, lifting above her sunglasses, and her partner put a hand on her shoulder. "We know that, Agent Lyons. We just can't—"

"You can't let a VIP just walk around without so much as a guard."

"I understand your frustration," he said, "but we can't just sit on her. She would be angry if we tried to do that."

And this is why you two were barely able to hold onto your jobs, Nicky thought. She had no idea what was going on with the secret service, but they were clearly becoming too lax. She wouldn't make the same mistake as these two.

"We had the whole area surveyed," the man said. "We…we weren't that far off, just far enough to make her feel like she was alone."

“You had the whole area surveyed?” Nicky asked, raising an eyebrow. She found that hard to believe, considering Natalia had vanished into thin air.

“Everywhere except the sea,” said the female agent. “But it’s a private beach. There shouldn’t have been any boats.”

“She was a VIP,” Ken said. “What made you think you could just let her walk around by herself?”

“Like I said,” the man continued, “she’s—”

“Did you even check on her?” Nicky said. “You could have been watching her the whole time, but you left her alone. I’m sorry, but that’s unacceptable.”

The two agents looked down, ashamed. Nicky could spend all day berating them, but she already knew the VP was doing a good job of that. She sighed, realizing that chastising them was pointless; they needed to focus on the case and work together now to get to the bottom of it.

“Forget that,” Nicky said. “Do you have any idea what happened to her? Any at all?”

“We don’t know for sure what happened,” said the woman. “But she wasn’t a good swimmer. She had a few near drownings when she was younger. I’d be surprised if she went near the water.”

“Okay, so she didn’t swim off,” Nicky said. “Do you have any idea who might have done this? Did Natalia have any enemies?”

“Or the vice president?” Ken offered.

“There might be some,” he started, “but I can’t think of any off the top of my head.”

Nicky looked at him sternly. “You’re assigned to protect her, correct? And you let her go off on her own. You can’t be sure of anything at this point, is that correct?”

“Okay, okay,” the man said, raising his hands. “But she was not a threat to anyone. She wasn’t a threat at all.”

“So you’re saying,” Nicky started, “that you have no ideas as to who would want to kidnap Natalia? No one who could have wanted her for ransom or—”

“I have a list,” the female agent cut in. “There are a lot of people who might want to hurt the vice president. But not many who might have something against Natalia herself.”

The other agent looked wary.

“Agent?” Nicky asked.

"I'm just not as sure as Agent Thomas," he said. Nicky realized then that she didn't even catch their names, but the short woman—that was Agent Thomas. If Nicky wanted to get along with them—as irresponsible as she thought they were—she figured it was better to play nice.

"Agent Thomas," Nicky said. "I just realized we never introduced ourselves. I'm Agent Nicky Lyons of the FBI. This is my partner, Agent Ken Walker."

The secret service agents nodded.

"Agent Laura Thomas," said the woman.

"Agent Scott Turner," said the man.

"Right," Nicky said. "Now that that's out of the way, Agent Turner, why do you not agree with Agent Thomas?"

"To be frank, I think it's possible she ran off," said Agent Turner.

"You think Natalia ran away?" Ken asked. "Why would she do that?"

"Because of pressures about her family," Agent Turner said.

"What pressures?" Nicky asked.

"The vice president is going through a bit of a scandal," said Agent Thomas. "His approval rating is down, and he's under more pressure than ever before."

"Because of the emails," Nicky clarified.

They nodded. Nicky had heard that VP Cavazos had some emails leaked showing that he had no intention of pulling out of big oil when he told the public that he would. Nicky wasn't surprised by this; it was typical of politicians to play both sides.

"Natalia's not that deep into her father's life," Agent Turner said. "At least not outside of the cameras. She...she wouldn't know that much about it."

Nicky considered this. The VP was having a crisis of some sort. That much was true. But Natalia's disappearance couldn't possibly be tied to that. She had no part in it. Not yet, anyway.

"That's all you have?" Nicky asked. "That he's having some sort of drama right now, and that would make Natalia run off? She's the daughter of a seasoned politician, and on top of that, Steven Cavazos and his family have owned stock in big oil for years. The family is no stranger to controversy, so why would she run off now, just because the VP's approval rating is down?"

Agent Turner looked down. "We don't have any evidence to tie it to the case."

"But you're thinking it," Ken said. "There's a reason you have this theory."

"Hmph," Agent Thomas said. "We have to explore all options in every case. We have to consider any and every possibility. It doesn't mean I believe it."

Agent Turner gave a small smile.

"Still," Nicky said. "You can't go off baseless theories alone. What would make you think that?"

"She hasn't been herself lately," Agent Turner said. "She's withdrawn, she doesn't want to go out anymore."

"Yes," Agent Thomas said. "She's become almost a different person."

Nicky considered this. If Natalia was really going through some sort of depression, that would explain why she had been pushing her security away.

"How long had she been asking you to keep your distance from her?"

"A few months," said Agent Thomas. "She used to want us everywhere she went, but slowly she started rejecting the idea. I even caught her on the phone once, telling a friend that she didn't want security on her anymore."

"So it's been building for a while," Nicky said. The two agents nodded. Nicky frowned. This was a good lead, but she couldn't follow it. There was nothing she could do to determine if Natalia's personality change was caused by something in the recent past or if it was just a part of her nature. Either way, everything seemed to indicate that she ran off of her own accord, which didn't make any sense to Nicky. If she was depressed, why run away? Unless she wanted to take some time for herself, but that didn't seem likely either. She would have just taken a vacation. It didn't make any sense.

"Okay," Nicky said. "Well, we want that list of names either way." She placed her hands on her hips and scanned the beach. It didn't seem like she was going to get any answers here, not yet.

It was time she investigated the scene of the crime herself.

CHAPTER FOUR

Nicky made her way up the beach, feeling every pair of eyes involved trained on her and Ken. Surely, news had spread that they had been specifically chosen for the case, and she wondered what everyone was thinking.

As she scoured the sand, looking for clues, she absently said to Ken, “I guess we’re taking a break from the list.”

“Yeah, well,” Ken said. “This is a bit of a big deal.”

Nicky glanced over her shoulder at him. Ken was wearing a loosely buttoned shirt—clearly, he’d been in a rush to get here too. She couldn’t help but think of the moment they’d shared on the beach only yesterday. He’d wrapped his arm around her, and Nicky recalled feeling like they were the only two people in the world. It was strange; Ken Walker was her partner, and Nicky wasn’t one to...develop feelings for men. But it still weighed on her, even with everything going on. Surely, she couldn’t actually be thinking anything romantic about Ken. That would be too far. Too unprofessional. Still, she couldn’t help but wonder if he’d felt it too.

She refocused on the beach, looking for any clue that might lead to what happened to Natalia.

“You have any ideas on what’s going on?” Ken asked, a note of concern in his voice.

“None,” Nicky said. “But someone has to have an idea. I just hope the list we have is long enough to cover everyone who might have a vendetta against the vice president’s family.”

“I guess so,” Ken said. “I don’t like the idea of Natalia being out in the middle of nowhere somewhere, though. I mean, we didn’t think the kidnapper would want her dead, but what if we’re wrong?”

“We’re not,” Nicky said. “Nothing about this screams out murder yet. She was taken by someone, not killed here. And if she did just run away, why leave behind her cell phone and purse? Like the vice president said, she’s a young woman...she wouldn’t be caught dead without her phone.”

Standing on the shore, Nicky looked out at the endless sea. The secret service agents had said that they'd had every bit of the resort covered.

Everything except the sea.

"Natalia knew how important it was for her to be safe," Nicky mused. "She wasn't going to run off on her own, not if she thought she was putting herself in danger. Her father is the vice president. She knows what she's worth, so why would she be so careless?"

"Right," Ken said, making his own way down the beach. "But maybe it's like that agent said. Maybe that's why she disappeared."

"Right," Nicky said. "But again, if she'd run off, she would have done it with her phone and purse. She wouldn't just leave it behind."

"So, she left on the beach, and she didn't leave alone."

"Yup," Nicky said. "Either that or someone else took her." She wondered if Natalia had been given a choice.

Probably not.

This definitely smelled like a kidnapping to her, not a runaway.

She peered out into the expanse of the ocean. No boats were in sight, which was odd. Every island had a dock, and the Xayana Resort was no exception. She would have expected there to be a few boats out here at the very least.

Despite the rough waters, it wasn't uncommon for people to go out on the sea. With so much empty space, it was a common hobby for the wealthier guests. They could sail out on the water or just relax and lounge around on their own boat. There was plenty of privacy out there. Plenty of places to hide, just as there was on the island itself.

No, Nicky thought to herself. Someone could go out on the sea and then come back, and no one would be the wiser. There was no way to know whether someone had done just that until after they had returned.

Still, everything seemed to lead back to the water. Nicky kicked off her shoes.

"What are you doing?" Ken asked.

Ignoring him, she stepped into the cool, shallow water. If there had been any footprints here, they were long washed away. A strong gust of wind blew in, sending Nicky's brown hair flying in all directions.

She was looking for something. She just didn't know what.

"Nicky, what are you doing?" Ken asked again, this time coming closer to her.

"I don't know," she said truthfully. "But I feel like I need to be in the water."

The tide was strong today, and the waves were crashing against the shore. Nicky walked farther in, not caring that her clothes were getting soaked. She needed to find something.

Suddenly, her foot hit something metal.

She bent down and retrieved it from the water. It was a small metal cap—maybe from an outboard engine? But it was painted bright orange, which Nicky had never seen before.

"Lyons, what is that?" Ken called out, coming to stand beside her.

"I don't know," she said, turning it over in her hand. "But I'm going to find out."

There were two people who were around Natalia the most—or were supposed to be around her. Nicky sloshed back to shore, Ken following. They both had wet feet now, but they made their way across the beach where Agent Turner was still with Agent Thomas, standing next to palm tree. She needed to see if they recognized this thing. She walked right up to them and held out the piece to Agent Turner, and his face took on a confused expression.

"What is it?" he asked.

"I don't know," Nicky said. "I found it in the water. Is it Natalia's?"

Agent Thomas came to stand beside them. She looked from the piece to Nicky, and then back again. "Where did you find that?"

"In the water," Nicky said. "I found it when I was walking along the shore."

"Wait," Agent Thomas said, examining the piece. "This looks like..." She looked at Agent Turner, wide-eyed. "Doesn't he…?"

Agent Turner nodded, and Nicky shot them a frown. "You two recognize this?"

"I don't know for sure," Agent Thomas said. "But Natalia's boyfriend, Matt, has a speedboat that he painted orange—very similar to that color."

"And that looks like it could be a gas cap from the same type of boat," Turner added.

"I didn't know she was dating someone," Nicky said, glancing at Ken, who looked equally confused.

"It was a recent development," Agent Thomas said. "The vice president didn't know about it, but it was only a matter of time before he did. He disapproved of them dating."

"Why?" Nicky asked. "Was there something about Matt he didn't like?"

“No,” Thomas said. “It’s just...Natalia’s father has always been very protective of her. He’s a politician, and Natalia has been in the public eye since she was born. He wouldn’t want her dating anyone unless the man was worthy enough to be the vice president one day.”

Nicky nodded. She could understand where the vice president was coming from, even if she couldn’t personally relate. Nicky’s own father was so absent from her life, he couldn’t have given less of a damn if she’d dropped dead, let alone who she was dating.

Still, a boyfriend her dad didn’t approve of, and now evidence that his boat might have been here…it was odd. Maybe Natalia just ran off with him. Maybe they were jumping the gun on this whole thing.

“What type of guy is Matt?” Nicky asked. “Why would the vice president disapprove? Was he too average? Not from a rich family?”

“No, nothing like that,” Agent Turner said. “I think it was the opposite, actually. Matt is from a wealthy family, but the vice president didn’t like the fact that none of the Callens would ever want to be president or even get into politics. They’re just happy to be rich.”

“And that’s bad why?”

“Because the vice president wants what’s best for Natalia,” Agent Turner said. “And that’s a man who would make a great president. Someone who’s willing to do whatever it takes to get what they want. There was actually an incident a few weeks ago—the vice president was having a social gathering at his Florida estate, and Natalia insisted on bringing Matt. We knew it was a bad idea, but…”

Agent Thomas cleared her throat, taking over. “Matt ended up getting drunk and causing a scene, then he was forcibly removed by the vice president’s security. Natalia was very upset.”

Nicky’s eyes met Ken’s. She could tell he was thinking the same thing as her.

Could Matt have done something brash, something to prove that he was strong, or something to stand up to her father?

Maybe he took Natalia to prove himself or get revenge. That was the worst-case scenario. At best, Natalia ran off with him, which was also a possibility.

“Do you know where this Matt guy is?” Nicky asked the agents.

“Natalia mentioned he was staying at another resort not far from here,” Agent Thomas said. “I think it’s called The Residence.”

“Which one is that?” Ken asked.

"It's just past here," Agent Turner said, pointing to the left. "About a mile and a half, give or take. If you walk along the shore, you can't miss it."

Nicky nodded. "Thanks." She turned to Ken. "Let's go."

CHAPTER FIVE

Nicky and Ken headed off in the direction Agent Turner had pointed in, and Nicky felt her nerves pinch inside her chest. She wasn't sure what to expect from Matt, but she could imagine the embarrassment a young man like him would've felt being forcibly removed from the vice president's home. She could imagine the rage, the revenge he might have formed in his mind.

Maybe Natalia had even suggested they break up over it. If that were the case, then his plot to kidnap her might make sense.

They walked down a rough path. It was hard to walk on, but they could see the other resort in the distance, sticking up into the air.

It was smaller than the Xayana Resort, more intimate in the sense. The resort was only two stories, with a little jutting out over the water. The white, sand-colored walls were a stark contrast to the blue sky and the green leaves of the palm trees surrounding it. The resort looked like something that should be on the cover of a travel magazine.

"This place is so beautiful," Ken said, looking up at the blue sky. "I can see why Natalia would want to come here. Being stuck inside your dad's house all the time must be suffocating, even if you are the vice president's daughter."

Nicky nodded. "A privileged position, but that doesn't mean it's always fun for her." She had to admit, it was possible that Natalia had run off, but she still didn't buy that. Matt would hopefully have more answers.

He better have more answers, especially if it was his boat.

They exchanged a look, and Ken nodded, giving Nicky a reassuring smile. It was a simple gesture, but it meant so much to Nicky. It was like Ken was saying, *I'm here for you,* and that was exactly how she felt. Like he was her rock.

They walked along the narrow beach path and up the small set of steps to the resort's front entrance. It was like a little slice of paradise. There was a little hut off to the side, where people could check-in when they came.

Once they reached the resort, they found the lobby. The spacious room was lit from within by a multitude of candles, and the late afternoon sun streamed through the glass doors that opened onto the garden. The candles cast a flickering glow over the stark white of the marble floors and walls, which were covered in golden reefs. The effect was overpoweringly bright, yet serene.

"Hello there," a woman said, sweeping her brown hair back as she stood behind the long desk. She had a friendly smile. "How can I help you?"

"We were wondering if Matt Callen was here," Nicky said, leaning forward so she could look at the woman's badge. "We were hoping to ask him a few questions."

Nicky then flashed her FBI badge, and the woman's eyes widened.

"Oh," she said. "Right. Well, Mr. Callen's room is on the second floor. Room 215."

Nicky and Ken exchanged a look. "Thank you," Nicky said, and she and Ken headed for the stairs.

They walked up the stairs, their footsteps echoing in the empty hallway. The resort was strangely quiet. It was a Thursday afternoon, and Nicky would have expected it to be busier.

They reached Matt's door and Nicky knocked, but there was no answer. She waited a few moments before knocking again, harder this time. Still no answer.

"That's strange," she said, frowning. "He should be here."

Ken shrugged. "Maybe he went out."

Nicky took out her phone, where she'd had a picture of Matt Callen sent to her. He was a generic-looking young guy—Nicky was only twenty-nine herself, but Matt was twenty-one, and the older she got, the more guys like him started to look the same: beach blond hair, tanned skin, dimples.

"We can look for him by the pool, maybe," Nicky said, "or the beach."

"Or the bar," Ken said, glancing at the photo. "He looks like a bit of a party animal."

Nicky nodded, tossing her hair back. "Let's go. I'm getting thirsty."

They walked along the hallway, past more sea-blue walls and golden reefs.

They found the bar, which was right next to the lobby. It was long and sleek, with a mirror running along the wall behind it.

The bar was busy. To Nicky's chagrin, there was nobody who looked exactly like Matt Callen, although there were a lot of people who were similar. None of them had his dimpled smile.

"Can I help you?" the bartender asked. He was a tall, muscular guy, with blonde hair that was slicked back with gel. He was wearing a tiny, black tank top and a pair of tiny, black shorts.

Nicky flashed her badge. "We're looking for someone," she said. "Matt Callen. You know him?"

"Matt Callen?" The bartender asked. "Yeah, he's here. He's at a pool party. It just started." He pointed to the back of the resort. "You can't miss it."

Ken and Nicky nodded and headed for the back of the resort, but once there, they saw that it was pretty empty.

Most of the guests were inside at the bar or hanging out at the pool. The view outside was stunning—across the water you could see the Xayana Resort in the distance.

A dozen people were lounging around, drinking and chatting. There was laughter everywhere, and the pool was a gorgeous blue, with golden tiles at the bottom. Nicky's toes were already beginning to prune.

"Are you looking for someone?" someone asked.

Nicky glanced up and saw that a girl was standing next to them. She had a tiny, silver bikini on, and her tanned skin shone like gold in the sunlight.

"Are you looking for someone?" she asked again, looking at their faces. Clearly, Nicky and Ken were out of place here.

"Yes," Nicky replied. "Matt Callen."

The girl's face broke out into a smile. "Right," she said. "Of course. He's just over there."

She pointed to the pool, where a boy was lounging in a chair, sipping a beer.

Nicky's heart began to beat a little faster as she looked at him. It was definitely Matt, and he was lounging around as if his girlfriend wasn't missing.

"Thanks," she said, and she and Ken walked over to the pool.

Matt was wearing a pair of dark green swim trunks, and he was leaning back in a chair with his feet up on the edge and a beer in his hand. His eyes were closed, but Nicky noticed that he wasn't asleep, just lying there and listening to the conversation in the pool.

"Why am I always the one to do all the work?" someone was saying, a guy with gelled spikes of blond hair.

"Are you seriously complaining?" a girl in a very tiny bikini said. "Why don't you get drunk, like the rest of us?"

Someone else laughed, but not everyone was laughing. The boy in the chair opened his eyes, and when he saw Nicky and Ken standing there, he sat up straighter, putting his beer down on the little table beside his chair.

"Hi," he said, giving them a smile. "Are you looking for me?"

"Are you Matt Callen?" Nicky asked.

"Uh, yeah, what's up?"

Nicky held up her badge. "FBI. We need to talk to you about Natalia Cavazos."

The people around Matt looked around, shocked, and started whispering. Did they not know he was dating the vice president's daughter? If that was the case, then Nicky could rule out the idea that Natalia had just come here to hang out with Matt. She really was missing. And if Matt took her, and was now trying to cover that up, then Nicky would get to the bottom of it.

"Uh, okay..." Matt stood up, glancing at his friends. Nicky gestured off to a small patch of grass off the property, a spot where they could speak in private.

Matt shrugged at his friends and followed her.

Nicky began walking, and Ken fell in step beside her. Matt, a few steps behind, glanced between them. His face was tinged with red, and Nicky could only imagine how he felt—he had just been pulled away from a pool party he was supposed to be having fun at. She looked for any sign of rage on him, any sign that this could trigger him to remember when he was removed from the VP's home. She saw nothing but nervousness on his face, though.

"So," Nicky said, after a moment. "You're dating Natalia Cavazos."

Matt nodded. "Uh, yeah, I guess."

"Got a picture?" Ken asked, his voice dry.

Matt reached into his pocket and pulled out his phone. He flipped through a few pictures, then handed it to Ken. Ken glanced at the screen, then handed it to Nicky.

She glanced at the picture. It was a selfie, with Natalia and Matt in the pool. Natalia was wearing a tiny, blue bikini, and she was leaning back, her wet hair slicked back, her face flushed and happy.

"You two are close," Nicky said.

"Yeah," Matt replied. "We've been dating for a few months now. Why?"

"How long have you known her?" Ken asked.

Matt shrugged, his eyes darting back and forth between them. "A few months."

"A few?" Ken pressed. "Three? Six? What is it?"

"Shit, man, I dunno. Seven?"

"And you're aware that Natalia was reported missing this morning?" Nicky asked.

Matt's face went pale. "Huh? No! Where is she?"

"That's the thing, Matt," Nicky said. "We don't know where she is. We're hoping you can help us."

"Well, I dunno where she is," Matt said. "I've been here all day."

"When was the last time you saw her?" Nicky asked.

Matt thought for a moment. "Yesterday afternoon, I guess. I took her out on a boat. She loved it."

The boat...it could be the boat that had a piece of it missing, left at the spot Natalia was last seen alone, without Matt.

"How did she seem?" Nicky asked.

Matt hesitated. "Okay, I guess. She seemed fine. She wasn't in a better mood yesterday morning. She's been a bit moody lately in general."

"Yesterday morning?" Nicky asked the question casually, but her heart was pounding. There was something about that morning that had been bothering her since she'd heard about it. She was starting to get a very bad feeling about it.

"Yeah," Matt said, nodding. "She was really hungover, and she wouldn't get out of bed. I had to force her. She was nice about it, but she didn't really want to go."

"Where did you go?"

"To the beach. I got her a fruit smoothie, and she kind of...chatted with me. She was cool, though. It wasn't anything weird or anything. Then she said her dad would be pissed if he saw us hanging out, so she took off."

"Did she say anything about where she was going?"

"She said she was going to Xayala Resort. I was supposed to text her to meet up without her dad finding out, but honestly, she was being a bummer so I just...forgot."

"Right," Nicky said. None of this quite implicated Matt yet, and there was a chance he'd have a solid alibi. But still, he was acting nervous and fidgety, and the cap from his potential boat was found at the scene...

"Do you mind if we see your room?" Nicky asked.

Matt leaned away and scratched at his neck. "My room? Why? I mean, we don't have to go there, it's so far..."

Nicky narrowed her eyes. What was he hiding?

"We'll be quick, Matt," she said. "Please, if you wouldn't mind."

"I…uh…I don't think that's a good idea," he said. Matt hesitated, glancing back at his friends. They were standing around the pool, chatting, but all of them were looking in this direction.

Nicky glared at him more. She didn't know what his plan was here, but she had a bad feeling about it.

Then, before she could even blink—

Matt made a run for it.

CHAPTER SIX

Nicky's breath caught. Matt bolted, bursting into a sprint. The grass was slippery and wet, and he almost lost his footing a few times as he ran out of the pool area and toward the winding, narrow road that led away from the estate.

"Hey!" Nicky shouted, jumping over the pool and sprinting after him.

She raced after him around the resort, tearing through the grass and trying to close the distance between them. Behind her, Nicky heard Ken running after them.

Matt was fast, and she was having a little trouble keeping up. He was running toward a gate leading to the water park area, and he shoved it open, running out. Nicky swore under her breath and picked up her speed, running faster than she ever had before.

Then Matt veered off past a splash pad, bare feet on concrete, running toward the water slides.

A feeling of dread filled Nicky's chest. This place was a maze and way busier than she'd realized. There were kids around.

People around. If something happened...

Matt was dodging around groups of kids and parents, weaving through the water slides and leaping over a child's pool. Nicky's heart raced. She was closing the distance between them, but she couldn't just tackle him in front of all these people.

Matt turned at the end of a row of water slides, and just before he did, he swept his hand over his eyes, as if to brush away sweat.

She had to catch him.

Matt ran past the main water slides, running to the smaller ones tucked at the corner of the water park. He was trying to lose her in the sea of people, and it was working. People were stopping to stare: some pointing, others calling out. Maybe Matt thought he could lose them in the chaos, but Nicky wasn't about to let him get away.

He reached the edge of the water park, but just as he was about to run across the concrete, he slipped.

Matt fell to the ground, tearing his knee open on the concrete. He let out a cry of pain, his hands gripping his knee as he rolled over onto his back. The weight of the impact drove him into the concrete, and he let out another cry of pain.

Nicky slowed down. Ken closed the distance between them, sliding in and coming to a stop beside her. They looked down at the boy lying on the ground, both breathing heavy with exhaustion.

"Get up," Ken said.

Matt didn't move. He just stared at them, his eyes watering up.

Ken grabbed him by the elbow and dragged him to his feet.

"Whoa hey!" Matt protested.

"What were you trying to do?" Ken asked.

Matt's eyes darted back and forth between them. "I don't know what you're talking about."

"Matt," Nicky said, "we know Natalia's disappearance wasn't an accident. We found a piece from your boat near the shore she was taken."

Matt's eyes widened. He opened his mouth, then closed it again.

"Say something," Nicky snapped. "Do you know something?"

"I..." Matt swallowed. "I don't know what you're talking about. Natalia's just been acting weird lately. I'm worried about her. What are you saying happened to her?"

"Take us back to your room," Nicky demanded. She wasn't buying this whole clueless act.

Matt held up his hands. "Okay, okay, I'm coming. But I don't know...I don't know anything about Natalia. I didn't do anything to her."

"Is that right?" Nicky said dangerously.

Matt glanced at her, and then back at Ken, and nodded. "It is."

Nicky didn't believe him for a second. "Let's go."

***

Nicky followed Matt through the resort and back to his room, with Ken right beside them. Matt walked back with them in silence. He didn't run anymore, but he still kept his head low and tried to avoid eye contact.

Matt unlocked the door and walked in. This was the first time Nicky and Ken had been inside, and Nicky was immediately hit with the smell of pot and stagnant beer. They took a moment to look around as he flicked on the lights. The place was a wreck—beer bottles everywhere, white dust on the glass coffee table that Nicky could only assume was cocaine.

Several pizza boxes were spread out on the floor, and there were even a few empty beer bottles on top of the television. This place was a total mess. And if this was how Matt kept his room...

"I don't know why you're so put out about this," Matt said, "I just smoke weed. That stuff isn't even that bad."

"We're going to search your room," Nicky said.

"What? No, you can't do that. That's...that's against the law. You can't do that."

"We can, and we are. Sit down on the bed and keep quiet."

Matt backed away, shaking his head. "I'm not sitting on that thing. There must be bedbugs or something."

"Matt, sit down," Ken said.

Matt didn't move. "I'm not—"

"Sit down on the bed," Nicky said, "or we'll make you sit on the bed."

"You can't do that—"

"Matt," Nicky said, "sit down on the bed."

Matt's eyes widened. He swallowed, glancing between them muttering, "Fine," and plopped down onto the sheets.

Matt was sitting on the bed, his fingers nervously tapping. Nicky nodded at Ken, who took the signal to stay and watch Matt while she looked around. Nicky slipped down a short hallway and peered into the bedroom, which, like the rest of the place, was trashed.

No sign of Natalia.

She checked the bathroom and the other bedroom too, but Natalia wasn't in the hotel room.

Nicky turned and found Ken standing in the doorway between the living room and the bedroom.

"Anything?" she asked.

"Nothing," Ken said.

Nicky walked back into the living room. She looked around, her eyes on Matt. She dug out the gas cap they'd found on the beach out and showed it to him.

"Do you recognize this?"

Matt shrugged. "I dunno, man."

"Where's your boat, Matt?"

"It's docked down at the beach."

Nicky nodded. "Show us."

Matt stood up. "What? Why do you need to go see my boat?"

"Because you're going to have to identify that gas cap we found on the beach," Nicky said.

"Maybe I don't know anything," Matt said.

Nicky glared at him. "You're going to have to identify that gas cap."

Matt swallowed. "It's at the beach."

"That's more like it," Nicky said.

They left the room and made their way through the resort, and then they were out in the open air. The sun was starting to set, casting the sky in a nice deep blue. The beach was ahead of them, and the water was still, a calm midnight blue. Their footsteps crunched on sand, and the waves were loud enough to nearly drown out the sounds of families chatting in the distance.

Matt led them to the beach, and sure enough, there was his boat, docked just offshore. Just like the agents had said, it was painted orange, a unique color for a speedboat.

Nicky glared at Matt and then started walking toward the boat. As she approached, she could see that the boat was a mess—the bottom was damaged, and there were dents in the side. It was also covered in bird shit.

Nicky glanced at Matt. He was shuffling his feet, his eyes on the ground. She stepped on the boat and looked around.

She didn't see anything out of place, but there was definitely something strange about this boat.

"Hey, be careful," Matt said, "that's my boat."

The wind was blowing, and the boat rocked in the waves. Nicky looked over the side of the boat, where there should have been a missing gas cap.

But it was right there, in place.

Nicky took out the gas cap they'd found at the beach. It was definitely similar, could even be from the same model of boat...

But it wasn't from Matt's boat.

He was innocent.

Nicky said nothing. She turned around and walked off the boat. She heard Matt sigh behind her.

"I didn't do it," he said.

She looked back at him. He had his hands in his pockets, and he was staring at the sand.

“I don’t know what you think happened,” Matt said, “but I didn’t kidnap Natalia.”

“Count your lucky stars,” Nicky said. She turned and walked away from him, back toward the resort.

“Hey!” Matt said. “Hey!”

But Nicky didn’t look back. She paced away, letting Ken handle Matt. Nicky heard Ken tell Matt, “You’re free to go for now, but make yourself available for questioning in case we need you.”

With that, Ken followed Nicky, who was too busy trying to figure out what had happened to Natalia. Was this guy involved? Or was this the work of someone else...someone trying to frame him. And even if it wasn’t, how could someone take her without being seen? She was the vice president’s daughter, damn it—how the hell did this happen?

Nicky didn’t know. But if Matt Callen was innocent, then she was back to square one.

CHAPTER SEVEN

Natalia kicked upward, her foot colliding with something hard and metal—the back of the truck. She couldn't see a thing, but she could feel the rumble of the vehicle beneath her, trapping her and carrying her off to only God knew where.

The truck must have turned, for now it was going downhill. Her hands were burning as they scraped against the edge of the truck. She kicked again, but all it did was send pain reverberating through her legs.

She had to get out of here. But how? Who had taken her? She hadn't gotten sights on her assailant—she'd only woken up in this damn cramped space with no clue what was going on.

She was the vice president's daughter, damn it. They had to let her go.

She wasn't worth anything to them. They could just let her out. This was kidnapping. This was—

Her heart was beating rapidly, and she took in a deep breath as though she could make the darkness not so dark. But all it did was send more dust into her mouth, and her throat began to burn.

It had to be the kidnappers. They had to have been watching her.

Nausea rose in her stomach, and she fought to keep it down. She couldn't throw up here—she couldn't do anything in this damn box. She was trapped, she was dirty, and she was running out of air. Her hands were quickly losing feeling, and her head was spinning.

Natalia felt her head hit the truck again, this time with even more force than before. She couldn't keep this up. She had to calm down.

They probably just wanted money. They would try to ransom her to her father. There was no way they'd kill her or hurt her...right?

Fear constricted her heart.

The thought of her father finding her like this made her stomach sink. He'd be heartbroken. He'd be so mad—she'd be so mad if this had happened to him.

She gulped back tears. She had to stay calm. She needed to think.

She took in a deep breath of the dusty air, but it didn't give her clarity. It only made her panic more.

Was he going to take her out?

Was this finally it?

She needed to get out of here. She needed fresh air, she needed to see her father, she needed—

She couldn't die like this. She couldn't die in this box. She couldn't die from suffocating. She couldn't die with no light and no air.

She had to calm down. She had to think things through.

They had to let her out sooner or later, right?

She'd just have to make sure she was prepared for it.

But what if? What if they were planning on killing her?

Or worse—what if they were planning on selling her off?

Natalia imagined herself being trafficked and assaulted—so many horrible things flashed through her mind. And this all started to feel too real. She thought of Matt, her boyfriend, who she desperately wished was holding her right now. They were supposed to meet up, but he never texted. For a moment, she closed her eyes and pretended they were together.

She let herself be in the moment with him—they were back at the hotel, laughing and making love. It was a happy memory that would outshine any other horrible ones they would create while they held her in this truck.

But then the memory shattered, and she was in the truck again with nothing but the sounds of her own breaths echoing through her ears.

She thought of her father, who she wished could protect her now.

She thought of her mother, who was too far away to save her. She thought of her friends, and how they would react when they found out. She thought of her life, and how it was going to change.

She needed to get out of this box.

She banged on the top of the truck, screaming as loud as she could.

"Let me out!" she cried. "Please let me out!" She screamed, banged, and kicked, but she was only rewarded with more pain.

She whimpered. "Let me out."

She felt the truck turn around, and she felt the vehicle descend.

Natalia shook her head, trying to get these negative thoughts out of her head. She was only making things worse. She was only scaring herself—she didn't need to be scared right now. She needed to be prepared.

She slowly reached upwards, blindly searching for something, anything, that could help her. Her nails scraped against metal, and she frantically felt around, trying to find something to anchor herself, or some kind of latch that could open this damn trunk.

But there was nothing.

She was trapped.

And right now, there was no escape. All she could do was pray. Pray someone would save her before it was too late.

CHAPTER EIGHT

Nicky sat at a table at the local police station, where she and Ken had claimed a temporary office. Ken sat across from her, sipping a coffee that he'd taken from the lobby, but the sour look on his face suggested that it wasn't great.

Sighing, Nicky leaned back in the chair and closed her eyes, trying to get into the head of someone who would risk kidnapping the vice president's daughter.

No one had claimed responsibility yet. There were no ransom requests. And the news didn't know—not yet.

The boyfriend theory had quickly dissolved, and Nicky knew now that they needed to look at that list the secret service agents had sent over. But where to even begin? The vice president of the United States could have a lot of enemies. Maybe this was to hurt him. Or maybe it really was just about the money.

"Ken," she said, opening her eyes, "do me a favor, will you? Run all the usual security checks on anyone who's ever been on the list. Just the names. Don't say anything. I don't want it to look like we're investigating them. Just run the checks, and then I'll decide what I want to do about it."

"How do you want me to run them?" he asked, not looking happy about it.

"Just do it. I'll tell you what to look for as I work through them," she said.

"Okay," he agreed reluctantly, taking out his laptop. "You're the boss."

Technically, she still was, as Chief Franco hadn't said anything different. Although this was the first time the task force Nicky was leading would be looking into someone who isn't on the top ten list of missing women. Obviously, the vice president's daughter had to take precedent, although Nicky still worried about the other people on that list.

She still worried about Rosie too.

Chief Franco had told her that if she could get some information...something concrete... then the FBI could reopen the case of Rosie Lyons. But it didn't seem like that would happen any time soon. Nicky couldn't blink without another case falling on her lap.

"What's up?" asked Ken, staring at her from across the table.

"What?"

"You keep looking at me," he said, frowning.

"Sorry," she said, pulling her eyes away. She forced herself to concentrate on the case at hand. "I was just...thinking. Any hits on the list?"

Ken looked back at the laptop. "Nothing concrete. The list is huge. I feel like if we were going with the ransom theory, someone would've claimed it by now, yeah?"

"Mmm," Nicky agreed, looking back at the papers on the table in front of her. She'd been through most of them. The list had included the names of dozens of the vice president's political enemies and an even longer list of online commentators who were outspoken against him. Ken worked silently on his laptop, no doubt running all the usual security checks on the list of names. Nicky gave herself a moment to process everything that was going on.

Most of the names on the list were politically involved in one way or another. Some of them were wealthy businessmen, others were athletes, and a few of them were actors. One of them was a comedian.

Nicky had been through the list twice already. There was nothing that stood out. No motive and no clues. The vice president's enemies were not necessarily enemies of the US, they were just enemies of the vice president.

But maybe the motive had nothing to do with the vice president. Maybe it was just about the money, and the vice president was just a victim of circumstance. In that case, maybe this wasn't about hurting anyone. Maybe it was just about getting rich.

For some reason, the idea of a kidnapping for ransom not being about hurting someone made Nicky feel a lot safer. For the vice president's daughter, at least.

His daughter...

Natalia. Nicky hadn't taken much time to think much about Natalia herself, about who she was as a person. Clearly, Natalia had been trying to forge her own identity separate from being the VP's daughter—Nicky could only assume that was why she'd insisted her guards keep their distance from her. She wanted to feel alone and independent.

Natalia probably had enemies too.

A sudden hunch struck Nicky. It seemed unlikely—but what if this wasn't about the VP at all?

What if this was about Natalia?

"Did Natalia have any enemies herself?" Nicky said out loud, and Ken looked at her, perplexed.

"Maybe...those secret service agents should know."

Nicky took out her phone. She had both Thomas and Turner's numbers. She called Turner first, and he picked up almost instantly.

"Agent Scott Turner," he said.

"Turner, it's Lyons," Nicky replied.

"Any luck on the list yet?" Turner was eager to ask, Nicky could tell. The sooner the FBI located Natalia, the more secure Thomas and Turner's jobs would be. If they never did find her, or if they found her dead...Nicky was sure Turner and Thomas would be kicked out of the secret service.

"Not yet," Nicky said. "Actually, I'm calling for something else. Did Natalia have any enemies?"

"I'm not sure what you mean," said Turner. "We're supposed to be looking for anyone who wants something from her."

"Yeah, I know," Nicky said. She hesitated, trying to choose her words carefully. "What I mean is, did she have any enemies who might want to hurt her, other than the ones her father might have?"

"You mean personal enemies of Natalia?" He went quiet for a moment. "It's possible. Let me talk to Thomas. We'll send you a list."

"I'll need a list of everyone Natalia has pissed off over the past few years. Friends, enemies, whoever," Nicky said. "And Agent Turner. Be quick."

"We will. Thank you, Lyons," he said. He hung up the phone.

Ken was staring at her with wide eyes. "What is it?"

"I'm not sure yet," Nicky said, toying with her phone. "But I'm wondering if this has anything to do with the vice president at all."

"What?" Ken said, frowning.

"Maybe this is about Natalia," Nicky said. "She's quite the rebellious girl, isn't she? The VP's daughter. She likes to do things her own way. Maybe she pissed off the wrong person."

"You don't think she was kidnapped for ransom?" Ken said. "She's the VP's daughter. Someone could still come forward."

"So, she's worth more than some random girl," Nicky said. "It might not be that simple. Until we get a request for ransom, then we can't rule anything out."

Nicky leaned back, anxiously checking her phone for an update from the secret service. The moment they had that list of names, they could narrow down their search.

"Damn, this guy is a piece of work," Ken said, typing at his computer. Nicky straightened up.

"You have a hit?"

"Not exactly," he replied, turning the laptop toward her. Nicky swiveled in her chair to his side of the table, looking over his shoulder at the file.

"Frank Grainger," she said, reading the screen, which showed a picture of an over-weight, deranged-looking man in front of the American flag. If she had to guess, it was a screenshot from a video, not an official police file.

"Real radical commentator online," said Ken, reading off the file. "He's never outright threatened the VP, but he's made his opinion very known, and the FBI has him on a watchlist for a reason."

"Anything else?"

"This guy is definitely anti-government," Ken said. "He's mostly just a blogger, but he thinks that the use of drones to spy on people is a violation of their rights. He's even gone so far as to get tiny drones of his own and have them fly around the NSA offices. He's a real piece of work."

"So, the FBI has a file on him," Nicky said.

"Obviously," said Ken.

"What else do you know about him?" Nicky said.

"He's a complete conspiracy theorist," Ken said. "He thinks he can see UFOs flying in the sky and that the government has aliens locked up in Area 51. He also thinks the government is using gyro technology to control our minds."

"Sounds like a real winner," Nicky said, looking back at the picture. The man had a thick beard and brown eyes that were full of hate. "What's his following like?"

"Actually, it's strong—really strong," Ken said. "Over four million online."

Nicky let out a whistle. "So, people are buying what he's selling."

"He's been trending online," Ken said. "Everyone who stumbles upon him becomes a believer. His popularity is growing. And he's only getting worse, the crazier he gets."

Nicky nodded, taking this in. Right now, this Frank guy was nothing but a man screaming at a camera. There was no reason to believe he could pull off kidnapping the VP's daughter, especially if he was already successful.

Just then, Nicky's phone buzzed. She eagerly opened it—and it was an email from Agent Turner. She opened it up, her heart pounding.

It was the list.

And it was alarmingly short—only about twelve names.

A note from Agent Turner read: *Natalia didn't have many enemies.*

Nicky could see that. She read from the top to the bottom. None of the names stood out to her—one did mention that a girl named Gina Fiore was one of Matt's exes, and she was upset that Matt was dating Natalia.

But near the end of the list, one name stood out.

Nicky had to read it twice to make sure her eyes weren't playing tricks on her.

The name was Frank Grainger.

"Holy shit, Walker," Nicky said. "Grainger's on this list too."

"No kidding," Ken said.

Nicky grabbed her laptop and slid it over, so she and Ken were working closely, side-by-side. She went to Frank's video page.

His last upload was a day ago, before Natalia went missing.

It was a video titled: *MORE CAVAZOS LIES? FAMILY DRAMA, PAMPERED DAUGHTER, AND MORE!*

Nicky couldn't believe it. Being on the VP's list alone wasn't enough to incriminate this guy over the others on the list—but being on both Natalia's list and her father's, it was too much of a coincidence.

"Walker—"

"Already on it," Ken said, typing into his laptop. He pulled up Grainger's last known address.

It was only a few hours away.

CHAPTER NINE

Nicky hit the road right away, comfortable behind the wheel of her car with Ken in the passenger seat. They whipped down the highway, headed straight for Frank Grainger's house, which happened to be along the water, in a small community called The Cove.

As she drove, Nicky mentally listed everything they knew about Grainger. She turned right on the highway, heading east toward her destination. They knew he was an anti-government conspiracy theorist and YouTube sensation who hated the Cavazos administration—and he was the only one on the VP's list who had a noticeable following.

It was a big leap to assume that he had something to do with Natalia's disappearance, but there were too many coincidences. He could easily have his boat on the dock by his house and could have made his way up the coast to Xayala resort to kidnap Natalia. It was all possible...but first, Nicky had to get there.

As she drove, she could feel Ken's presence beside her. He was quiet, and she wondered what he was thinking about. It really was only yesterday that they'd finished their last case. The emotions had been high...maybe that was why he'd wrapped his arm around her. Maybe that was why she felt a sudden, strange connection to him that she hadn't felt before.

It was strange. She wondered if he was thinking about the same thing.

As Nicky was driving, Ken was reading up on Grainger more, so Nicky asked, "Learn anything useful?"

"I don't know. Maybe it's best to learn it from his own mouth."

Nicky was about to ask Ken what he meant when a sound started playing from his phone. It was music—the national anthem—followed by a voice.

Frank Grainger's voice.

"Hello, everyone, and good morning to all you awakening wolves out there. I'm your host, Frank Grainger, and this is The Honesty Report."

Nicky and Ken exchanged a look. Honesty. Right.

The podcast went on: “Today we’re looking at our favorite liar...our favorite political liar. That’s right, Vice President Steven Cavazos is our hot topic today, and we can’t get enough of the bullshit coming out of that guy’s mouth. I know it pisses you all off as much as it pisses me off.”

Nicky shook her head, rolling her eyes. Ken didn’t smile, but his lips twisted into a sneer.

“Okay, let’s get started,” Grainger said. “With all the controversy swirling around him, he’s been on the radio trying to clear his name. And he’s been using his daughter to sway public opinion. He’s using his daughter to get sympathy. It’s bullshit, isn’t it?”

Nicky glanced over at Ken and saw that his face had gone stone-cold.

“His daughter,” Grainger continued, “Natalia Cavazos, is not a victim here. She’s a criminal, actually. Anyone with that much money has gotta be a criminal. She’s a daddy’s girl with no talent. That’s right…and she’s a liar. She’s spread lies about me, in fact! Those screenshots she posted on her fancy little social media page—calling me a stalker and a creep? They were fake! I never messaged her, I never called her hot…”

“This must be what the feud was about,” Nicky said. “This is why he’s on Natalia’s list.”

“Yeah,” Ken said, pausing the podcast. “Apparently Natalia’s social media followers went after Grainger after he aired this. Natalia herself never interacted with him other than posting the screenshots of an alleged message from him.”

“Maybe that’s what pissed him off,” Nicky said. “Maybe he’s making a statement to her followers.”

“Maybe,” Ken said, turning his phone off and pocketing it. “But right now, it doesn’t really matter. We’re only interested in one thing—finding that kid.”

Nicky couldn’t help but notice that Ken used the pronoun kid when talking about Natalia. Not girl, not woman—kid. She understood exactly why. Natalia was a grown woman, but she was also the VP’s little girl.

They drove the rest of the way in silence, ruminating over the case. Finally, she turned into the development. Tucked away, but still close to the water, was the community of homes. Grainger’s home was right on the water—a brown, suburban looking house.

Nicky pulled into the driveway, parking behind a black SUV.

"Apparently, being a conspiracy theorist pays these days," Nicky muttered.

"You could say that," Ken said back. "How should we do this?"

"By the books," Nicky said. "We'll knock, ask some questions, and see how he reacts."

Ken nodded and they got out of the car. Nicky could feel the warm breeze blowing through her hair and the sun beating down on her back. Nicky walked up the driveway, trying to see if the curtains in the front window were moving. But she couldn't see a thing.

At the front door, Ken rang the doorbell three times, and Nicky could hear the piercing sound echoing through the house. But no one answered.

"Frank Grainger?" Nicky called, knocking hard. "This is the FBI. Please open up."

The two of them stood in front of the door, waiting. But no one answered.

Suspicious, considering there was a car in the driveway...

"Might as well look around the property if he's not answering," Nicky said.

"Good idea," Ken said.

They walked around the house to the backyard area. There was the brown wooden dock, leading out into the water.

"Just like the video," Ken said.

Nicky nodded, approaching the dock. There were two boats docked there—maybe Frank had a third?

"Watch the left one," Nicky said. "Let's see if it has a name on it."

Nicky walked over to the right boat. It was a small yacht, about thirty feet, with a white and red stripe on the side. But there was no name on the front.

To the right was a small powerboat about the size of a jet ski. There was a name, but all the paint had been rubbed off. It was just a smooth, white surface.

"Interesting," Nicky muttered. She ran her finger over the top, checking the paint. It was just as smooth as the rest. Someone had sanded and cleaned the name off.

Why would they do that? Maybe they'd removed an outer layer of orange paint.

"Let's see if any of these are missing gas caps," Nicky said.

Ken nodded, and they both got to work, checking all three boats. But none of them were missing gas caps. Nicky checked the two larger boats, and nothing looked suspicious.

Still, Nicky had a weird feeling about this guy. Really weird. The feud with Nataila's father and her social media followers...it was very possible he had kidnapped her to make a grand statement of his own.

And there was still that SUV in the driveway.

"Let's check the house again," Nicky said.

"Back door?" Ken asked.

"Yeah," she said.

They walked around the house, checking in the windows. Nicky kept expecting to see Frank Grainger sitting on the couch, watching them. But no one was there.

"Frank?" Ken called. "This is the FBI. Please open up."

But again, the only one who answered was the echo of the doorbell.

They tried the back door. Locked. Then they tried the garage. Locked.

"I'm starting to get a really bad feeling about this," Ken said.

"Me too," Nicky said back.

"What do you want to do?" Ken asked.

"Let's look around one more time," Nicky said. "Maybe we missed something. Maybe he's hiding..."

As Nicky was saying it, something—like a presence—compelled her to look up.

And in an open window on the second floor of the house, someone was peering through the curtains.

"Shit—he's here," Nicky said, her heart jumping into her throat. "He's hiding from us."

Then, the barrel of a shotgun pointed out from above.

"Duck!" Nicky yelled, pulling Ken out of the way. The shot never fired, but they had more than enough reason to enter. "Come on," Nicky said, taking off for the front door. "Let's get inside."

Nicky took out her gun and shot the deadbolt three times, then kicked the door open.

"Clear!" Ken called, once he'd run in after her.

They both ran through the house. Nicky could hear the echoes of her footsteps clicking on the tile.

"Frank Grainger?" Nicky called. "This is the FBI. Please come out with your hands up."

They checked the first-floor rooms. Nothing. But, as they did, they stepped into a spacious foyer and admired the floor-to-ceiling windows that overlooked a manicured lawn. Tapered, wooden doors flowed from the foyer into the rest of the house, which seemed to be outfitted for elegant living. They peered in through the frames of these French doors and saw the living room, a dining room with a polished wooden table, a kitchen with stainless steel appliances—none of which were in use and all of which were spotlessly clean—and a den, which was piled high with family photos.

They went up the stairs, checking each room. They were halfway through when Nicky noticed that the door to the attic was open.

“Shit—he’s up there,” Ken said.

“Go!” Nicky ordered, standing at the foot of the stairs.

Ken rushed up the stairs, and Nicky followed. She watched as Ken flung the door open and climbed the ladder inside.

Gun drawn and pointed to the ceiling, Ken stepped into the attic. Nicky heard Ken breathing hard, his feet smashing down on the insulation.

But as their eyes adjusted to the attic, that was when they saw it: Frank’s video setup. The American flag. It all happened up here, in the attic, while the rest of his house was beautiful luxury.

Nicky was really starting to think this guy was just a massive conman.

“Frank, we know you’re up here,” Nicky said.

“We just want to talk.” She waited, listening.

Then, she heard it. A shuffle. Maybe a moan.

Ken looked at her, signaling with his eyes. He was going to go left. And she would go right. It was an old game they’d learned in the academy, and they’d played it before.

Ken took a deep breath and stepped toward the sound.

Just then, Frank ran out from behind a pile of boxes, shouting: “Get out of here, deep state freaks!”

He charged right at Ken, but he dodged, and Frank fell face-first onto the ground. He scrambled to his feet and yelled, “I’ll never talk,” Frank said, his voice wavering. “Not to the FBI, not to the CIA, not to the NSA, or the deep state or anyone else. I’ll never talk—I’ll be a man of my word!”

He charged at them again, but this time, they were ready.

Nicky tackled him to the ground, pulling his arms behind his back while Ken cuffed him.

CHAPTER TEN

Nicky dragged a cuffed Frank Grainger downstairs and shoved him onto his leather couch (which was admittedly gorgeous). Nicky and Ken stood, arms crossed, looking down at a trembling Frank.

"You can't do this to me!" Frank shouted. "I have rights!"

"We are the FBI," Nicky said. She didn't have time for this shit. "We have questions, and you're going to answer them."

"I have rights," Frank said, over and over again. "No one can lie to me. I have a right to remain silent!"

Nicky had to be tactful with this. She couldn't outright ask Frank if he kidnapped Natalia because if he didn't, he could leak it to the press, and then Nicky and Ken would be in for a world of shit. No, she needed to find a way to see if he was involved in this without tipping him off.

But how?

She figured it was best to start with the only piece of evidence they had: the gas cap. Nicky pulled it out of her pocket and showed it to Frank.

"Do you recognize this?"

"What? No!" he screamed. His face contorted with anger. "You damn fools, get out of my house! You don't have a warrant!"

"You assaulted two federal agents," Ken pointed out. "Better not play that game, buddy."

"You can't scare me!" Frank said, standing up and walking toward Nicky. "I'm a patriot, goddammit! I'm not afraid of you!"

He was getting really close.

"I can do whatever I want, and you can't do anything to stop me!" Frank said.

Nicky shoved him back on the couch, and Frank fell down onto his ass. With his hands bound by the cuffs, there really wasn't much he could do, and that was starting to settle in for him. He gave them a begrudging look.

"I was someone who fought for my country," Frank shouted. "I'm not some lowlife, like you. I fought for something real. Not for some stupid cause you deep state idiots dream up in your room."

Nicky ignored him—like in his videos, Frank was just spewing into the void. “Are you sure you don’t recognize this?” she pressed.

“It’s a gas cap,” he said. “What do you want me to say? What the hell do you want from me?!”

“We just want to know if you know anything about this,” Nicky said.

“I have power,” Frank said. “I have influence. I have friends. And I will never, never talk to the FBI.”

“We’ve been through this,” Nicky said. “And we’re not going to move on until you come clean to us.”

“Come clean about what?”

Nicky shared a look with Ken. She could tell he was thinking the same thing as her—they needed to somehow get Frank to confess to the crime. They needed to get him talking, without blatantly stating why they were really there.

“You seem to have quite the obsession with commenting on politics,” Nicky pointed out.

“Yeah, because I get to stand up to bureaucratic shitbags like you,” he spat.

“Yet here you are, in this beautiful house,” Nicky said. “Your followers don’t know you live in such luxury, do they?”

He bit back his reply, shooting them a disdainful look. “What the hell do you want from me?”

“We’ve noticed you’ve been posting some...disturbing content online,” Nicky said. “Such content might implicate you in a crime, should something happen to one of the people you comment on.”

Frank looked at them, long and hard, for a moment, still with that angry face...until Nicky watched, in real time, as he let out a sigh and dropped his persona like taking off a damn mask.

“Look,” he said. Even the gruff tone of his voice had become smoother, more reasonable. “I’m not really like I am online in real life, all right?”

Nicky lifted an eyebrow, looking at Ken, who wore the same look. They weren’t wholly surprised.

“I’d never actually hurt anybody,” Grainger continued, “and to be honest with ya, I don’t even really care about any of these stupid political leaders I comment on. I just chase what gets the views...last year it was that one congresswoman. This year, it’s the vice president. Everyone’s pissed off at him, and I get views for it.”

Nicky and Ken shared a look again. They didn't really know what to make of this guy, but as long as he was turning over this much new information, it didn't matter.

"What about your videos?" Nicky asked.

"I'm just playing a character," Frank said. "I'm Frank, but I'm also the Patriot, and that content I make...it's, uh, it's all a lie."

Nicky didn't know what to make of that. She wasn't entirely sure how good of a liar this guy was, and she wasn't about to question his motives.

"I know people play characters online," she said. "But you seem to be taking it way, way too far."

"Hey, why's it matter, right?" Frank said. "I make content, they watch it. Everybody wins."

"You spread hate online," Nicky said, anger growing in her. "It could embolden someone to do something drastic. Don't you get that?"

"Look, I'm not responsible for what people do," Frank said. "Even if they do listen to me, they're still responsible. I couldn't stop someone from going and doing some nonsense…and I wouldn't want to." He was still pretending to be this badass, but Nicky could tell the façade was crumbling. "I'm not a monster. I'm just a guy trying to make a living in this world, okay?" he said. "So, whatever you feds think I did...I didn't do it."

As much as Nicky didn't want to admit it, she was starting to believe him. Plus, his boats weren't missing their gas caps. They had nothing on him right now.

Still, Nicky had to cover her bases. "Where were you this morning between eleven a.m. and noon?" Nicky asked.

"I was doing a livestream on my second channel," Frank said. "It's more lowkey, not many people know about it. It's for my real fans. There should still be a recording up there. I didn't do anything to anyone."

"What's the channel called?" Ken asked, taking out his phone.

"Patriot Truth," he said. "Go ahead and check. I was streaming from my attic for four hours today. Took live calls and everything."

Nicky and Ken shared a look, and Ken pulled up the Patriot Truth channel on his phone. Sure enough, there was a video posted from that morning, and Frank Grainger was in it, with a dozen comments by followers. It was timestamped, proving his whereabouts.

There was no way he was the one who kidnapped the vice president's daughter.

"Are you gonna take these cuffs off me now?" Frank asked. "Yo should be lucky I'm not pressing charges."

"If we find out you're lying," Ken said, "we don't need a warrant to come back here."

"Yeah, yeah," Frank said, "it's all fun and games until somebody loses an eye."

Nicky nodded, and Ken undid the cuffs. Frank rubbed his wrists, and then rubbed his hands over his face.

"What was this all about, really?" he asked. "I mean, I know what it's really about. But you've got to tell me—what the hell did you really think I did?"

Nicky didn't know how to answer, and before she could figure out how, Ken put it into an easy-to-digest version.

"We can't disclose that information now, and we'd rather just put this whole thing behind us."

"We won't charge you for assaulting us if you forget the whole thing happened," Nicky added.

Frank let out a sigh. "Guess that works out. Doesn't really matter now, does it? Now, get out of house."

Ken and Nicky turned to leave, but Frank called after them. "And don't go spreading this all over the internet," he said. "I've worked hard to get my reputation. I'm not gonna let you ruin it."

They ignored him and left his house. Frank Grainger was a shitbag in Nicky's eyes, but he didn't kidnap Natalia.

All that meant was that someone else did.

CHAPTER ELEVEN

Natalia took in a deep breath of the dusty air, but it didn't give her clarity. It only made her panic more. They were still driving along, and it felt like it had been hours that she was in the dark, cramped trunk of his truck.

Terror squeezed at her heart. She wanted her dad. She wanted her boyfriend. More than anything, she just wanted to see the light of day again.

She never should have been such a brat to those secret service agents her father had hired...if she'd just let them be close to her, then they could have protected her.

Now, she was going to die, be trafficked, or worse.

She closed her eyes, unable to bear the nothingness any longer. Somehow, she just knew that her life was about to change forever, and not for the better. It all felt like a surreal dream.

Natalia thought about the life she'd lived so far. The mistakes she'd made that had led her here.

Maybe if she hadn't been so determined to be a grown-up, she would at least still have her dad.

Now, she didn't know how to turn things around. She'd burned all her bridges, and though she had years of freedom still ahead of her, it felt like it was all coming to an end.

When Natalia looked back on her life, she would remember this day.

What a miserable way to go. Maybe she deserved it.

Maybe she should have listened to her dad when he told her not to date Matt Callen. If she hadn't, then she wouldn't have been so determined to be alone on the beach so she could sneak Matt over. But he never even came. He never texted. He was supposed to meet her, and he never did...

Maybe he didn't care about her after all.

Natalia's eyes stung. She wondered if Matt would give a single damn that she was taken. That she was going to die.

She doubted he'd come to save her.

But her father...the vice president...he would. Someone would. Natalia had to believe that. It was the only thing that kept her going.

She didn't know what was worse: the thought of her dad knowing she was gone or the thought of him not caring.

At least if he didn't care, she wouldn't have to live with the burden of that knowledge. It would be easier to die if her dad didn't care.

That's the thing about the human psyche. It wasn't about logic as much as it was about emotions. It was about feelings.

And feelings were a lot more powerful than logic.

Even if Natalia was mad at her dad, and sometimes wished he'd just leave her alone, she couldn't bear the idea that he didn't care what became of her.

She wouldn't be able to live with that.

Natalia reached up to gently touch the backs of her hands to the tears on her cheeks. She was sniffling, and she was so weak that she couldn't stop the tears which fell down her cheeks.

She was going to die.

The truck slowed, and Natalia felt her heart race. What was happening? Were they here?

The truck stopped, and the engine died.

Please, please, please let me live. If I get out of this, I'm never going to be so stupid again. I've learned my lesson. I know now how dangerous life can be.

She tried to imagine what it would be like to be rescued.

She tried to picture her father's face and his arms when he wrapped them around her. She tried to imagine what he would say when he found her.

She tried to picture Matt, too, but all she could see was the look on his face when she'd kissed him goodbye.

He hadn't even had the decency to pretend to care.

She probably did deserve to die, but if she could just have one more chance to make things right, to be the person her father wanted her to be...

Please, God. Let me live.

Natalia heard voices outside, their words indistinguishable from one another. It was all she could do to hold herself together. She wanted to cry, to scream, but she couldn't do it. She had to be strong.

She thought she heard a car door open and then close, but she couldn't be sure; her sense of sound was muted in here.

Another sound. Someone was outside. They were moving around. She couldn't make out anything more than that.

The truck began to rock back and forth, as if someone had gotten in or gotten out.

What was happening?

Was he going to take her out?

Was this finally it?

She needed to get out of here. She needed fresh air, she needed to see her father, she needed—

The trunk suddenly burst open, flooding her eyes with light, and she wanted to scream, she wanted to claw her eyes out, she wanted to do anything to make the light stop.

She covered her eyes, but it was too late. She couldn't see anything but white light.

"Stop!" she screamed. "Let me go!"

But the light just kept getting brighter and brighter. It seemed to fill every inch of her world, burning into her skin and searing through her mind. She could hear herself screaming, but it felt like she was miles away.

Her eyes began to adjust, and she could feel her body being lifted up, dragged painfully by her arm.

She tried to look up at her assailant—but all she saw was a brown bag, coming straight toward her face.

Then, everything went black.

CHAPTER TWELVE

As the sun set, Nicky knew this was about to become another night spent away from her own bed—another night in a hotel, alone with Ken. She walked into their new hotel room and threw the key card on the table. Through the white curtains, the sunset created a warm glow over the sky. At least the view was nice.

She went to the table and immediately pulled out her laptop while Ken shrugged off his jacket, hanging it on a hook. The room was decent—two beds next to each other, a bathroom with a shower and jacuzzi tub off to the side. Ken sat down on the edge of one of the beds and loosened his tie while Nicky sat in the chair and pulled up the list of names.

Frank Grainger wasn't their guy. Then who was?

She wasn't sure which list to focus on—Natalia's or her father's.

She wasn't sure where to continue at all.

Nicky let out a sigh, taking a moment to think it all through. It was too strange. It'd been hours now since Natalia had gone missing, and still, no one had claimed ransom. The news hadn't broken the story either.

So, who took her—and why?

Was she even still alive?

Nicky had to believe that she was. Natalia hadn't even been missing for twenty-four hours, and she was the vice president's daughter—surely, whoever took her had to want something.

They wouldn't kill her, would they?

Nicky shook her head. She had to stop overthinking things. The truth was, Natalia was missing, and she was the agent in charge of finding her. She had to focus on the task at hand: finding out the story behind the story, then finding the girl.

She picked up her laptop and pulled up the list of names. Ken had already made it partway through the VP's list and had flagged a couple of names who could be worth looking into. Nicky started there.

"Want me to grab us some dinner?" Ken asked, walking over to Nicky to look over her shoulder. Her face heated up as she felt him get closer to her, and she caught a whiff of his cologne.

"Sure, that's fine," she said, trying to ignore the stuttering in her voice.

Ken left the room to get dinner, and Nicky started scrolling through the flagged names.

The list of flagged names was long, but it wasn't too hard to narrow it down to the ones who had a criminal record—a few names popped out at her.

Dennis Hartman. He'd been arrested for an armed robbery in his early twenties and got off on a technicality. He'd been in and out of prison two or three times since then. He was currently on probation from a DUI. He had an account online dedicated to slandering the VP.

Danny Parks. A three-time loser in prison for burglary and breaking and entering. He was out of jail for six months now, after serving a four-year bit for the attempted murder of a police officer. He was a guy who got arrested a lot and had never spent more than a year in prison at a time. He was working at a resort not far from Xayala, and he also had been vocally against the VP online.

All of these guys had been critical of the VP and had criminal records, but that wasn't enough to pin this on them. It was a huge jump from "critical of the vice president" to "kidnapped his daughter." She needed something more concrete.

She had to keep looking.

Nicky wasn't sure how much time had passed when she looked up and saw Ken walking back toward the room with a tray of food. She had a crick in her neck from leaning over her laptop, and she sat up as Ken walked over to her with the food.

"Thanks," she said, taking the food from him. She didn't realize how hungry she was until she started eating. She hadn't eaten much all day.

They ate in silence, with Nicky deep in thought and Ken focused on eating. She had to figure out something—anything—to get them moving forward with this.

"You've gone through that list of names twice," Ken said, setting down his fork. "Any luck?"

"Not really," she said. "It's just...I know that we don't have enough to incriminate any of these guys."

"Don't worry about it," Ken said with a shrug. "We'll make something. It's just going to be a matter of doing an in-depth investigation on each one."

“I know, but something’s bugging me,” Nicky said. “The people on this list, the ones with criminal records—they all seem like the type who would demand something for Natalia. Still, we have no ransom.”

“I know.” Ken leaned back in the chair, a perplexed look crossing his dark, thick brow. “We could still get one...maybe the kidnapper wants the news to break first?”

Nicky shrugged. It was possible. She still had a sinking feeling in her stomach, a feeling that something was off or missing.

“I still don’t know what the ransom demand is,” she said. “And we could get one. We could get one any minute.”

She dropped her fork and leaned back, looking up at the ceiling. There was nothing in her head except blur. She couldn’t see a way forward. Natalia’s father is the VP. She’s his only daughter. Now, Nicky’s the only one who could clear this up.

“I know,” Ken said, sitting up and picking his fork back up. “We’ll keep looking—”

“No,” Nicky said, her voice firm. “We don’t have time to keep looking for ransom with no one claiming it.”

They had to move. What would they do if this were a normal case, not the president’s daughter? Where would they start?

They would talk to the victim’s family first.

She stood up, walking over to Ken with her plate of half-eaten food. He looked up at her with a frown.

“What are you doing?” he asked.

“I’m coming up with a new plan,” she said.

“What’s the new plan?” he asked, setting down his fork and getting to his feet.

She was still forming it. “The last time we talked to the vice president—we didn’t get to talk much to him as a person,” Nicky said. “We didn’t get to talk to him much as Natalia’s father.”

“What do you mean?” Ken asked.

“I think we need to talk to the man again,” Nicky said. “We need to talk to the vice president.”

“I don’t know if it’s a good idea to talk to him right now,” Ken said. “We can’t let him know what we’re doing.”

“How do you suggest we do that?” Nicky said. “While we’re out chasing down leads, he’s still trying to come to terms with the news. He’s still trying to figure out how to keep his daughter from being the world’s biggest news story.”

She took a breath and looked back at her food. Her appetite had disappeared.

"We need to get back in there," she said. "We need to sit down and talk to him as a father—not as the VP. We need to get into his head, see how he's taking this, and what he knows."

"You're probably right," Ken said. "We need to do something different."

"Then we should go talk to him," she said, walking back to her food and setting it down on the table.

"What do you think he'll say?" Ken asked, picking up his plate and following her back to the door.

"I don't know," she said, sighing. "He's going to be pretty mad that we haven't found Natalia yet. I'm going to be mad at us, too, if we don't find her soon."

CHAPTER THIRTEEN

In all of her career, Nicky never thought she'd be knocking on the vice president of the United States's door. After getting through the adequate security, Nicky and Ken now stood on the door of the VP's Florida home. The sun had fully set now, and the stars were slowly emerging. The night was warm and humid. The vice president's home was regal. Its brick façade had brickwork resembling a Roman aqueduct. It was large and imposing: its windows were long, wide, and tall, and its front door was of the same width. The door, itself, was a dark stained oak.

Nicky raised her hand to knock on the door again, but it swung open before she could knock. Vice President Steven Cavazos stood on the other side, his gray hair mussed, and his face lined in worry.

"What did you find?" he asked. "Are you any closer to finding my daughter? Where is she?"

"Sir," Nicky said, stepping forward. "We wanted to talk to you—"

"What is it?" the VP demanded.

"We need to talk to you as a father," Nicky said, trying to keep her voice even and calm. "We have a few questions—"

The VP raised his hand and turned away from the door. "No, we don't have time for this," he said. "Why are you wasting time with questions? This is my daughter's life on the line."

Just as Nicky was about to reply—to ask him to please talk to them—a woman appeared beside Steven.

It was his wife, Marie Cavazos.

With brown hair curling around her face and warm eyes that glinted with mirth and a thousand other emotions, Marie held an elegance about her that Nicky had rarely seen in real life.

"Steven, calm down, please," Marie said, facing Nicky and Ken. "You're the FBI agents assigned to our daughter's case, right?"

Nicky nodded. "Yes, ma'am. I'm Agent Nicky Lyons, and this is my partner, Agent Ken Walker."

"It's an honor to meet you, ma'am," Ken added.

Marie smiled warmly. "Please, come inside."

The VP's wife turned and led them inside. As they stepped in, they were confronted by an understated opulence. The hallway was wide, lit by gem-like chandeliers that glinted in the light. The walls were a warm, deep green, and the floors were hardwood. The furnishing was simple and elegant.

Marie walked down the hallway, then stopped at a door. "I'll make some tea," she said. "Steven, you should relax. We need to give them time to talk."

"Sit down," the VP said, before his wife could speak. "We're going to find out what you're hiding from me."

"Sir," Nicky said. "We don't want to keep anything from you. We just want to talk about Natalia—"

"Sit down," the VP said again, pointing to the living room.

Nicky and Ken exchanged a nervous look before following Marie into the living room. The dinner table was still set up with plates, glasses, and silverware. The VP watched them with hard, angry eyes. Marie smiled sadly, leading Nicky and Ken over to the white couch, where they sat down.

Marie took a seat in a chair, while the VP hovered over his wife, standing behind her. Nicky couldn't help but think that he was acting suspiciously guarded, compared to their earlier meeting.

"Sir," Nicky said, clearing her throat, "we just wanted to talk to you, to try to get more information on what might have happened to Natalia."

"You should be out looking for her," the VP said. "Not sitting here in my house."

Discomfort radiated through Nicky. She looked at Ken, taking momentary comfort in his blue eyes. At least they were in this together.

"Sir," she said, after a moment, "we need to understand what you know about Natalia. We need to—"

"You should be out there," the VP said, raising his voice. "I want you to find her. I don't care about the rest."

"The rest?" Nicky asked.

"It's my daughter," he said. "Don't you understand that? She's out there, somewhere, and we need to find her."

"Sir," Ken said, his voice calm, "we need to get information from you to understand why we should be looking for her."

A moment of silence hung in the air, broken by the sound of a teapot whistling in the kitchen. The VP waited until he heard the sound of a cup being set on a saucer—likely a servant getting it ready—then walked into the kitchen, leaving them alone. Nicky stared at his back as he went. Why was he acting so strangely?

"What is it you want to know?" Marie asked, softly.

Nicky and Ken turned their attention back to the VP's wife. She was looking at them with an odd expression.

"Can you tell us more about Natalia?" Nicky asked. "What was she like? Were you close?"

Marie nodded, wiping at her eyes. Even in her distress, the VP's wife was still beautiful. Her brown eyes seemed to glint with a thousand emotions at once. "We were close," she said. "We were very close. She was my best friend."

"What did she like?" Ken asked. "What was she interested in?"

Marie smiled, her lips curving up slightly, as she leaned back. "She liked to read," she said. "She liked to read a lot. She liked to read books of all kinds. Natalia was very smart. She was a bright girl. She wanted to go to school—to get a real education. She didn't want to just be the VP's daughter. She wanted to be herself—to be her own person."

"What about her relationship with her father?" Nicky asked. "We were told that he didn't approve of her boyfriend, Matt Callen, but she continued to date him anyway."

"Yes," Marie said, her eyes widening. "She continued to date him anyway. She loved him. She was going to marry him. She was happy."

Nicky frowned. "There's a possibility that she's not actually in danger," she said. "There's a possibility that she's hiding—that she left intentionally."

"No," Marie said, her eyes widening further. "She wouldn't do that. She wouldn't leave without a word."

"Has Natalia ever run away before?" Nicky asked.

Marie nodded. "When she was younger, yes," she said. "A few times. She met a boy in high school, and she didn't want to admit that she liked him and that they were dating. She wanted to keep the relationship a secret, so she ran away. But she always came back eventually. She always came back."

"What makes you so sure?" Nicky asked.

"Because she's my daughter," Marie said. "She said she'd come back, and she always did."

"How do you know that?" Ken asked.

"Because I'm her mother," Marie said, her voice breaking. "I could tell when she was lying. I know my daughter."

She was crying again. Nicky was on the verge of tears herself. It was completely understandable: if you put any woman in that situation and asked them about their daughter, they'd probably break down.

But there were still questions to be asked. The VP came back in, holding a cup of tea.

"Vice President Cavazos," Nicky said, trying to stay professional. "Your wife tells us Natalia has run away before."

"Not for many years," he said, setting his teacup down on the console table behind him. "My daughter didn't run away."

"Sir," she said. "There is a chance that she ran away. In that case, we have to be very careful. If she's hiding, we have to make sure that we don't tip her off or scare her into running again."

The VP glared at her. "We don't need your help," he said. "I want you to leave this house, and I want you to not come back until you've found Natalia."

Nicky frowned. "Sir, I—"

"Leave," the VP said, raising his voice again. "I want you to leave right now."

Nicky and Ken looked at each other. That seemed to be the last straw. The VP's wife had been sitting quietly, but when her husband raised his voice again, she pushed her chair back and stood up.

"That's enough, Steven," she said. "The agents are not leaving until they have the answers they need to find Natalia!"

The VP glared at her, his eyes flashing with rage. The silence in the room thickened. Nicky could feel it pressing against her skull. She'd never seen a man of his caliber react like that before, and she didn't know how to interpret her feelings.

Nicky and Ken looked at Marie, shocked by her shouted words and sudden outburst. The VP's face turned red. His eyes flashed.

"Sit down, Marie," he said. "You won't talk this way to me in public!"

"I just want to find out what happened to our daughter!"

She was yelling. The VP was yelling. Nicky, for her part, was frozen to the spot. It was like a nuclear family meltdown.

"Marie!" the VP said, sharply. "You will sit down!"

"No!"

In front of the cameras, the Cavazos family always seemed so perfect. A classic American family. But Nicky could see now that they had their own marital issues—their relationship was on the cusp of an eruption, and she and Ken were here to witness it.

“I’m not going to let you yell at us the way you do!” Marie said. “I’m not going to let you tell us that we don’t understand!”

“I’m the Vice President!”

“I don’t care!”

The VP clenched his fists at his sides. Nicky could see his jaw muscles twitch. She didn’t know what to do—she couldn’t figure out what was going on. Was the VP frustrated that they weren’t doing a good enough job? But he wasn’t giving them any leads to follow...

“Marie,” he said, his voice low. “You will stop this right now. You need to think about the optics of this. You need to remember that you will be the First Lady one day. You—”

“I don’t care about that either!” Marie snapped. “I don’t care about that! Not right now!”

Nicky stood up—she couldn’t just sit here. “Sir,” she said, loudly, “we’re just trying to help out. We just want to find Natalia—we want to help you. We’re going to have to leave before we can do that.”

The vice president looked at Nicky, and in that moment, she saw something in his eyes: guilt.

Something moved in Nicky’s gut. A feeling. An instinct...

She had thought the VP was acting strange before.

But now she was certain of it.

He was hiding something.

“Please,” the vice president said, “go wait in the foyer while I talk to my wife.”

Nicky had no choice but to listen. But she wasn’t done talking to Steven Cavazos. Not at all.

CHAPTER FOURTEEN

Nicky faced Ken in the foyer of the Cavazos mansion, the chandelier shining above their heads. He had his hands shoved in his pockets, and he glanced over his shoulder into the room where the vice president was still arguing with his wife. They could hear their vague voices through the wall. Nicky had seen dysfunctional relationships before, but she didn't expect this from the Cavazos family.

Ken muttered to Nicky, "What the hell do you think that was about?"

"I don't know," Nicky said. She leaned closer to him so they wouldn't be heard, then looked up at Ken, meeting his eyes. "Walker, listen...I have to be honest. I know he's the vice president, but I think he's hiding something."

He looked down at her. For a moment, Nicky could feel the tension between them. They were close, close enough that she could smell him. It was a subtle, musky scent—something between wood and the sea. She glanced up at him again and saw that his eyes were locked on hers and filled with concern.

They were close enough that she could imagine what it would be like to kiss him.

Ken raised his eyebrows. "What do you mean?" he asked, his voice low. "What do you think it is?"

"I don't know," Nicky said. "I don't know what it is. But...I think it's something more than normal marital struggles."

"Like what?" Ken asked.

Nicky leaned closer to him. "I don't think he's telling the truth," she said.

"You're joking..." he said, his voice low. Then he sighed. He leaned closer to her and said, "Lyons, look—I've been following your lead this whole time, since we were paired up together. But I don't know if I can support this. Accusing the vice president of lying in his own home...this could go nuclear."

Nicky looked over at him, meeting his eyes again. She said, "I know. But I just have this feeling about it. I know it's a lot to ask, but I need you to trust my instincts on this one."

Ken looked down at her for a long moment. He sighed, looking away. "I can't say I have another option. What if you're right?"

Her heart swelled, and she was grateful that he was taking her seriously. Nicky was damn sure of her instincts on this one. "Thanks, Ken."

He nodded stiffly. "So, what are you thinking?"

"I think he's hiding something about his daughter. Something about where she is."

"Jesus Christ," Ken said. "That's explosive."

"I know," she said. "That's why we can't bring any of the other agents in on this. If we're right and we get the VP to admit that he's responsible for Natalia's disappearance, we're going to have to arrest him immediately and take him in. We can't risk leaking this to the press."

Ken shook his head. "That's just crazy," he said. "I don't care what political party you're in, that's just crazy."

"I know," she said. "I'm not saying that he kidnapped her, I just...I think he knows something. He's acting too strange."

"I have to agree with you there," Ken said. "So, what can we do?"

Nicky took a deep breath. This might end up being one of the most challenging moments of her career. She had to look the vice president of the United States in the eye and ask him, point-blank, if he was hiding something. But she had to get him alone, away from his wife.

"We need to split them up," she said, nodding toward the living room, where the VP and his wife were still arguing. "I want to talk to the vice president alone."

"How do you suggest we do that?" Ken asked.

Nicky looked over her shoulder, toward the living room. "Marie, the vice president's wife, is the key. You try to talk to her for a moment. I'll get the vice president to come out here so he's not in earshot."

"What should I say to her?" Ken asked.

"Just talk about her daughter," Nicky said. "Keep her distracted. Say you understand how much she cares about Natalia and that it must be horrible for her. Just keep her talking."

Ken nodded. "Alright," he said. "I'll try my best."

Nicky squeezed Ken's arm. "Thanks, Walker," she said. "I'm counting on you."

Ken gave her a look, but then he nodded, and they both re-entered the living room. The VP shot them a look, but Ken quickly said:

"Mrs. Cavazos, do you have a moment? I wanted to ask you something—it's about Natalia's relationship with Matt Callen."

"I can answer that," the VP cut in.

"Actually, Sir," Nicky said, "I wanted to ask you too. Agent Walker will talk to your wife."

The VP gave Nicky a cold look, making her stomach twist with nerves, but he nodded. "Fine then."

Nicky didn't give him time to change his mind. She gently placed her hand on his elbow and said, "Let's go into the foyer, Sir."

She led the vice president out of the living room and into the foyer. He was stiff, not making eye contact, but Nicky didn't care—she had to get him alone, and now. She had to try to get information about his daughter.

"I know what you're doing, Agent Lyons," he said. "You were just trying to split my wife and I up."

"I apologize, Sir," Nicky said. She wouldn't do him a disservice by lying; he was still the vice president, and no matter what, Nicky still respected him. But she needed to know what he knew... what he was hiding.

"I'm not going to allow you to try to interrogate me like that," he said. "I'm not going to let you—"

"Sir," Nicky said, "I'm not trying to interrogate you. But I do need to ask you a few questions."

He stopped walking, his back to her. "I don't have many answers for you," he said. "I'm sure you've realized that by now."

Nicky kept walking. The VP was about to turn and face her, and she didn't want him to do that. She didn't want him to see the look on her face.

She stepped closer to the vice president and took a deep breath. "Sir," she began. "I don't want to make accusations, but I think you're involved with your daughter's disappearance."

The VP whipped around and faced her. "What?" he said, his voice rising. "What the hell are you saying?" He looked around at the walls, as if expecting someone to be hiding in the shadows. He looked at Nicky with wide, terrified eyes.

"Sir, please," Nicky said, "just relax and let me ask you a few questions."

"No," the VP said, shaking his head. "Are you kidding? I should call security on you!"

"I apologize," she said, "but I had to know if you could tell me anything about Natalia."

"I can't tell you anything about my daughter," he said. "I have no idea where she is. I have no idea what happened to her. You can ask me whatever you want to, but I don't know anything."

Nicky could hardly believe what she was hearing. Her gut was telling her that the VP was hiding something, but she could be wrong. Maybe he really did have no idea. She stared at the vice president. He was tall, at least six-one, and an intimidating figure despite his older age.

But his eyes were cold. Rigid.

Nicky stared at him for a moment, trying to push past the coldness in his eyes. But she couldn't get anything past it.

She forced herself to ask the question. "But you are hiding something, aren't you?"

Their eyes locked. Nicky's heart was pounding into her throat, but she had to stay strong. She had to treat him as if he were any other man, and not the vice president of the United States.

He was silent for a moment. Then, he said:

"I'm sorry, Agent Lyons, but I don't have time for this. I have a fundraiser to attend. If there's nothing else, I'll have my assistant show you the way out."

"Sir," Nicky said, "I'm sorry, but I can't leave until you answer my question."

"I'm afraid I'm going to have to ask you to leave," the vice president said.

"How can you do that?" Nicky said, her voice rising. "You are hiding something, aren't you? You helped your daughter disappear."

"I did not help Natalia disappear!" the vice president said. "Now, unless you want me to call security, I suggest you leave."

"Sir," Nicky said, "I'm not leaving until you tell me what you did with your daughter."

The vice president's cheeks were flushed, his eyes wild.

"I swear to God," he said, "if you don't leave right now, I will call security and have them escort you out of here."

Nicky stared at the vice president, her heart pounding with fear. She was going to lose her job over this. If she didn't get out of there now, she would risk everything.

But Natalia was out there.

"If you don't know where she is, then she could be in danger," Nicky reminded him, her heart pulling. "Sir. Your daughter is in danger. I only want to find her."

That seemed to get through to him. The VP had a concerned, guilty look take over his face—the same guilt Nicky had seen earlier.

He did know something.

She just didn't know what.

"Sir, please..."

The vice president sighed. "Come to my office with me."

CHAPTER FIFTEEN

Nicky's heart leapt into her throat. She wanted to ask questions, but she knew she couldn't waste any time. She was sure that she was right. She was sure that she should trust her gut.

She followed him down the hall. The VP's assistant was standing by the doorway when they went back into the living room, and the VP said, "I'm going to my office to speak with Agent Lyons. Please excuse me."

Nicky stood by the door, listening to the assistant excuse the VP and go back to her computer. The VP led Nicky down the dark hallway to his office. They stood in front of the massive desk, and he motioned to one of the chairs in front of it.

"Sit," he said.

Nicky sat. The vice president stepped around the desk and sat down behind it. Nicky stared at him, her heart squeezing.

She could lose her job for this. Her whole career. Forget finding Rosie—Nicky might not even be an FBI agent anymore. But she had to stay strong. She had to fight.

"Sir," she said. "What did you do with your daughter?"

He looked into her eyes and said, "I did not kidnap my daughter."

Nicky stared into his eyes for a moment, searching for the truth. His eyes were cold, hard.

"But you did help her disappear," she said, pushing on. "You helped her cover up the truth."

"No," he said, shaking his head. "No...that's not what I'm hiding. Really, I know nothing about what happened to Natalia. But..."

Nicky's heart picked up. "But what, Sir?"

He was quiet, his face strained. Nicky's pulse fluttered. What on earth was he about to drop on her?

"Please, Sir," she pressed, "anything, no matter how small, could help us find your daughter."

He let out a breath. "Agent Lyons, you must keep this between us."

"Of course, Sir...only Agent Walker and I will know."

"All right." He clasped his hands on the table and leaned forward. "Agent Lyons, I have another family."

Nicky's heart leaped into her throat.

"What?" she blurted. "Another family?"

"Please, you must keep this quiet. If it were to get out, it would be a massive scandal. It would destroy my career forever. And my family."

Nicky stared at the VP, unable to believe what she was hearing. "Another family, Sir?"

The VP nodded. "I have an illegitimate daughter. Natalia's half-sister."

Nicky's head was spinning. Her stomach was turning, queasy. "Natalia has a half-sister?"

The VP nodded. "Yes. A brother too."

Her mind reeled. She didn't know what this meant for Natalia, for the case, but this was huge. Steven Cavazos, vice president of the United States, had another family.

"Does your wife know?" Nicky asked. "Does Natalia?"

"No." His face hardened. "Agent Lyons, let me remind you. If this gets out, I will have your badge. You understand that, right? You and Agent Walker will both lose your jobs. I'll see to it myself."

Nicky shook her head. No, he couldn't. "But—"

"I'm not kidding, Agent Lyons," he said. "I will not have this upend my political career. I'm going to run for president one day, and I can't have this get out. I'm trusting you to keep this a secret."

As much as Nicky didn't appreciate being threatened, this was the vice president. She nodded.

"I won't tell anyone, Sir," she said, her stomach in her throat.

The VP nodded and relaxed. "Thank you for your discretion, Agent Lyons. I'm counting on you. I trust this will never get out."

"No, Sir," Nicky said. "I promise, it won't. But...what about the mother?"

"I was getting to her," the VP said. "The mother is a woman I met years ago. She was a secretary at my old office, and it was years after I married Marie. She was...young. She was so beautiful and so innocent. I fell in love with her."

"You...fell in love with her," Nicky said, stunned. "So, what happened? Why aren't you with her?"

The VP sighed. "When I met her, I was a congressman, and she was just a secretary. I was being blackmailed, and when I told her, she offered to help me. She said she would help me if I gave her a job in a congressional office. She would be the assistant to one of the congressmen. I didn't think anything of it. Marie and I had barely been having sex, and I was lonely. So, I took her up on it. And for a year, everything was perfect. She was everything Marie wasn't. She was beautiful, she was exciting, she was funny, she was intelligent, she was...well, she was perfect. But then Marie got pregnant with Natalia. At the same time, the woman—Ainsley was her name—got pregnant as well, with twins. Natalia's half-siblings, who she has no idea about..."

The vice president paused, and Nicky took a moment to absorb all this. It was a lot of drama, but then again, no one ever really knows a politician. Apparently, not even his own wife.

"I couldn't have my wife know," the VP said. "She was having a hard time dealing with Natalia, and I couldn't have this to add to the stress. I begged Ainsley to have an abortion. She refused. She was adamant that she would have her children. She wouldn't even consider it. I respected her wishes, and she had the children. But I realized that I wanted a life with Marie, not Ainsley. A secret, pregnant girlfriend would ruin me. Ainsley...did not like that. She threatened to expose me, to expose us, if I didn't at least stay with her in secret. For all these years, I've paid for their lives. I've lived in fear that one day, it would be exposed, and I'd be ruined. As you know, the stakes are higher than ever now that I'm vice president."

"I understand, Sir," Nicky said. "But why didn't you tell Natalia? I mean, if you two were so close, then you really should have told her. You should have trusted her."

"I know," the VP said. "But I couldn't. I couldn't tell Natalia. I knew she wouldn't want to know."

"You shouldn't have kept it from her," Nicky said.

"I know," he said. "But I didn't want to hurt her. I also didn't want to hurt Marie. I love my wife, and I couldn't tell her. And I love my daughter. I didn't want to have to hurt any of them. I'm afraid I've hurt them all now. I'm so sorry."

Nicky shook her head. This was too much to handle. Too much of a secret for her to carry. But Nicky would take it to the grave if she had to.

Nicky nodded. "I understand, Sir. Your secret is safe with me. There is only one thing that matters to me here: do you think your other family could have anything to do with Natalia's disappearance?"

"I'm...I'm not sure. I tried calling Ainsley, but I didn't get an answer. Obviously, I haven't been able to go see her in person—there are too many eyes on me right now."

"What about the last time you saw her?" Nicky asked. "What was she like?"

"She was…well…Ainsley and I have always had a complicated relationship. I would say she wasn't any different than normal."

"And what is she normally like?"

"She's quiet but protective and very defensive."

"I understand," Nicky said. "I'll look into it. At least now we have something to look into."

The VP nodded, then pulled out a paper and wrote something down. He handed it to Nicky—it was an address. The two stood.

"Thank you, Agent Lyons," the VP said.

"You're welcome, Mr. Vice President," Nicky said, tucking the address in her pocket. With that, she reached for the door.

"Agent Lyons," said the VP, stopping her.

"Yes?" she looked at him.

"Please...look into this quickly. I want to find out what happened to my daughter, and I want to bring her home."

Nicky nodded. "I will, Sir. I promise. Let me get Agent Walker and we'll get started."

"Thank you, Agent Lyons," he said.

Nicky nodded and left, going downstairs to the main level, where Ken was still talking to a distraught Marie. Ken held a hand out to her, hovering it over her, but not touching, as though to safely reassure her. But when he saw Nicky coming into the room, he looked at her, saw the expression on her face—and it was like he could read her mind. He nodded at her.

They had more work to do.

CHAPTER SIXTEEN

Natalia gasped as she woke, surrounded by darkness yet again. But this time, wherever she was—it wasn't moving.

She felt cold tile beneath her. Confused and delirious, she rose to her feet on wobbly legs. It was dark, and she was in some sort of house. Moonlight seeped in through the windows. The house was small, but it was...nice. Cleanly furnished, no dust...

It didn't make any sense. She'd been kidnapped. And they'd taken her here?

Where were they?

It didn't matter. She had to get out of there. Get home. She stumbled toward the door.

In a distant part of her mind, as she made her way to the front door, she noticed a strange picture on the wall.

She stared at it as she limped across the room, barely paying attention to it until she was in front of it, staring at the portrait.

It was a portrait of her father. The vice president of the United States.

Natalia's heart jerked. What the hell was going on?

There was a kitchen off to her right, and on it, the stove read the time in neon green letters: 9:04 p.m.

Whose house was she in?

And where were they? Where did the kidnappers go?

Natalia didn't know. Frankly, at this moment, she didn't even care. She opened the front door, and to her surprise, she was free.

The house was in some sort of forest, and a road stretched into it, into the darkness of the night. Fear caught her for a moment. She'd have to walk out there alone, but it was better than staying here.

As she stepped out onto the road, she heard a car coming. It was a long way off, but she could hear it well enough. Hope dashed through her. It could be help!

Or it could be them. Her kidnappers.

She ran into the woods, hiding in the shadows.

She heard it slow down. There was a small driveway, and she heard it make a turn. The thought that maybe it was help after all overwhelmed her. She ran after it, but it was too late. It was gone.

She didn't hear another one, so she had no choice but to follow the road.

It was dark, and she had nothing but her bikini on. But that didn't matter. She had to get home. She'd figure out a way to get there.

She had to.

She found a road sign a little way off. It said "Rye, 1/4 mi."

Natalia sighed. It was a start.

The clouds were parting, and bright moonlight shone through. She could barely make out the road ahead of her.

The road stretched far into the distance, and she saw something at the end of it. A house. She'd reach it before she got to town.

She was still barefoot. She was still in her bikini. And it was still dark. She didn't care. She had to get home.

As she walked along the road, she found herself slowing down. She wasn't sure why. She didn't like being out there. Something wasn't right.

She could see the house ahead of her. A mansion. It was big, bigger than anything she'd ever seen before. It was a long way off, and she would've never thought it was there when she was driving. But now that she'd reached it, it was hard to miss.

It had a big wall around it. She could see there was a gate, but it was open. There was a sign at the entrance, but it was too far to see. There had to be someone, somewhere, around here who could help her.

In the distance, she heard what sounded like a car. She was sure this time. It was definitely a car, and it was coming her way. She ran toward the sound.

"H…hey!" She cried out. "Can you help me!?"

She waved her arms, hoping they'd see her. It started slowing down, and she started to run faster, her heart pounding in her chest. It was going to be okay. This was going to work out. She was going to get out of there. Everything was going to be alright.

The car slowed to a stop next to Natalia, and the windows rolled down revealing a man behind the wheel and a woman in the driver's seat. They were young and had brown hair and brown eyes, like her. They each wore strange, unnerving smirks, and instantly, Natalia was on edge.

"Hey there," the guy said. "You need some help?"

Natalia got a bad vibe from them and instantly regretted asking for help. "Um...no, sorry, I, uh, I thought you were someone else."

"You must be pretty cold wearing that out here," the girl said, a smirk teasing at her lips.

"No, I'm fine. I just need to get to town."

"We all do," the guy said, and they shared a look.

"Yeah," the girl said. "You look like you could use some help."

"Thanks, but I'm alright."

"I think you should let us help you."

Natalia bit her lip. "I told you, I'm fine."

"Hey, it's okay," the guy said with a kind, yet unnerving voice. "We'll help you."

The girl nodded. "Yeah, I'm sure you'll be much safer with us than out here alone."

Natalia backed away from the car. "Really—it's okay..."

"You don't have to be scared of us."

"We like you."

Natalia jumped as the girl opened the passenger side door. "I don't—"

"Come on," she said, "we'll make it fun."

Natalia turned and started running.

The girl got out of the car. "Come on, Natalia."

She had no idea what these people were doing there, but she had no time to think about it. She had to get home.

"Come on, don't be like that!" she heard them say. "We'll make it worth your while!"

"I said no!"

She ran faster.

"Don't be like that!" the girl cried out. "We just want to have fun!"

Natalia was barely listening. She had to get out of here. There was no way that she'd be able to make it all the way to the gate. If she could just get to the end of the road and cut across the field, she could make it home.

But the lights of the car appeared behind her. Chasing her.

"Natalia! Come on! We just wanna have some fun!"

She ran faster. The car was catching up to her.

"C'mon!" the girl cried. "We just wanna have some fun!"

"Not with you!" Natalia said, looking over her shoulder. The lights of the car were damn near blinding her now.

"It's not like we're strangers!"

"I don't even know your name!"

"Well, we can work on that!" the girl said with a laugh.

"No, I don't want to!"

"Give us a chance!"

"No!"

The car was nearly on top of her now. She could see the girl's eyes, glaring at her through the window.

It was too late.

Natalia ran as fast as she could, but the car was faster.

CHAPTER SEVENTEEN

The headlights of Nicky's car cut through the long, dark forest. It had taken them an hour to get there by car, and now Ken was quiet in Nicky's passenger seat as they drove. Ainsley Gibbons, the vice president's mistress, lived deep in these woods, apparently. It was a rich neighborhood, each house separated by acres of trees. Nicky could only assume the privacy was exactly what the VP needed to hide his other family.

"I still can't believe this," Nicky said as she drove them steadily through the night. "A whole other family. Damn."

"I know," Ken muttered, looking out the window. "We really can't let it get out."

"Never," Nicky said. "The vice president said he'd have both our jobs if we leak it."

Ken nodded. "Or worse."

"We'll make sure it stays contained."

"This is going to cause plenty of press..." Ken trailed off. "We can't let that happen, either."

"We won't."

The headlights swam through the darkness of the forest. The blackness of the shade had a way of swallowing up the light so that even though the car was moving quickly, it felt as if it was moving slowly. It seemed to take a long time to travel the narrow road, though really it only took a few minutes before she was able to see the edge of the trees.

As they drew closer, all Nicky could wonder was if Natalia would really be there. If the VP's second family was jealous of his "real" family, then that could be motive. Ainsley, herself, could be a prime suspect. The VP already described her as an obsessive woman, someone who wasn't afraid to blackmail.

"Maybe this Ainsley wants to use Natalia for leverage," Nicky said, thinking out loud. "Maybe she wants to use her to get the VP to come clean about their affair."

"If that's the case, why hasn't she come forward yet?" Ken asked.

Nicky chewed on her lip as she drove. "That's the question, isn't it? Who knows what type of woman Ainsley is?"

"Well, we're about to find out," Ken said.

Nicky pulled to a stop outside of the Gibbons' home and killed the engine. The house was regal and rich-looking with its towering columns and marble busts alighting the lawn like sentinels. The sky grew darker as the clouds advanced to block the moon. The house was aglow with lights from within. There were two cars parked in front of the house: one a rather expensive looking black sedan and the other a white Cadillac sedan.

Nicky and Ken got out of the car and walked up to the door. Nicky took a deep breath and knocked. The house—the whole forest—was eerily silent, eerily still.

Then, a set of high heels clicking on the floor beyond the door. The door opened to reveal a woman in a tight, long, maroon dress. Her hair was silvery blonde, and her eyes were as blue as ice, and she was holding an ice pack to her cheek—as if she'd just been punched.

"Can I help you?" she asked. Her voice was as cold as her stare.

Nicky flashed her badge. "I'm Agent Nicky Lyons with the FBI. This is my partner, Agent Ken Walker. Are you Ainsley Gibbons?"

She nodded, eying them warily. "I am..."

Behind Ainsley, in the house, Nicky could see a bookshelf had been knocked over, and there was shattered glass all over the marble floor. Concern grew inside her as her instincts kicked in.

"Is everything okay, ma'am?" Nicky asked, peering over Ainsley's shoulder.

Ainsley's eyes narrowed. "Everything is just fine."

"Are you sure?" Nicky asked. Her heart picked up. "Is someone in the house with you, Ms. Gibbons?"

"No," Ainsley said sharply. "It's just me."

Nicky could hardly believe this woman was trying to say everything was fine when she was in this state.

"Well," Nicky began, glancing at Ken, "do you mind if we come in? We need to ask you a few questions."

Ainsley gave them a long, cold look before she nodded, opening the door more.

Nicky and Ken followed her inside. The interior looked like a palace. The floors were covered in marble, and the walls were adorned with gold. The ceiling was painted with angels, and the air was rich with lilac. Two staircases on either side of the entrance hall led to the second floor.

But there was also the wreckage. A fight had clearly broken out here...but with whom?

Natalia?

"Ma'am," Nicky said, "if someone broke into your home, we need to know about it."

Ainsley paced back and forth. She was clearly upset about something. "I don't know what you're talking about," she said. "No one broke into my home."

She seemed to be hiding something. Or lying. Nicky wasn't sure which.

"What is this about?" Ainsley asked, her voice prim.

There was no use beating around the bush. "Ms. Gibbons, we know about your relationship with Vice President Steven Cavazos."

At first, Ainsley's face went pale. But then, Nicky saw what she swore was relief on her face. This was probably the first time in twenty years that Ainsley was being acknowledged for her relationship with the vice president of the United States.

"Did Steven send you?" Ainsley asked. A nervous edge took over her voice.

"Actually, we're looking into the disappearance of Steven's daughter, Natalia," Nicky said.

Ainsley should have been shocked to hear it. It hadn't hit the news yet. And Steven had said he hadn't spoken to her yet.

"Natalia is missing?" Ainsley asked, and Nicky sensed faux surprise in her voice.

"Yes," Nicky said. "Natalia disappeared from a resort earlier today. We're concerned for her well-being. And we thought you might know where she went."

"I'm afraid I don't," Ainsley said. "Why would I?"

"Well, with all due respect, ma'am," Ken interjected, "you have been living in Steven Cavazos's house for twenty years with his other family. It stands to reason that you might know more about the family than we do."

Ainsley's blue eyes flashed. "I resent that."

"Why?" Ken asked. "Are you just saying you don't know anything about the girl's disappearance?"

"I don't know anything," Ainsley said. "And I resent your accusations toward me. If you don't mind, I'd like you to leave my home."

Nicky shook her head, still full of suspicion. "Ms. Gibbons, we're not going to leave until we find out where Natalia is. We need to know that she's safe."

Ainsley looked very uncomfortable in her skin. "I do not know where Natalia is..."

"I don't believe you." Nicky crossed her arms, bracing herself against the cool stare of Ainsley.

"I'm not lying!" Ainsley's tone turned harsh.

"Who assaulted you, Ms. Gibbons?" Nicky asked.

"Nobody!"

Nicky wasn't having this. Something had happened here—and the stakes were too high to waste time questioning. She looked at Ken. "Walker, go look around."

"What—you can't do that!" Ainsley exclaimed.

"We can, ma'am," Nicky said. Ken didn't waste any time—he took off into the house, leaving Nicky alone with Ainsley, who was trembling.

"You…you can't do this," Ainsley said. "I have a right to privacy."

"Then tell me where Natalia is, and I'll call Agent Walker off," Nicky said.

"She's not here!"

Nicky breathed out through her nose and glanced around the room. The hallway they were in had photos on the walls. No pictures of the vice president, but many pictures of Ainsley with her children. Unlike her, they had brown hair and brown eyes—like Natalia.

"Walker!" Nicky called into the house. "Got anything?"

"Nothing yet!" he shouted.

"I am telling you, she's not here," Ainsley said.

Nicky locked eyes with her. If Natalia really wasn't here, that didn't mean the VP's "other family" was innocent.

"Where are your children, Ainsley?" Nicky asked.

Ainsley sucked in a breath. "They are out with their friends. Please don't bring my children into this."

"This is about their half-sister," Nicky said. "Do Marissa and James even know Natalia exists?"

Ainsley swallowed. "I've never told them about her."

"You've been keeping this a secret from them?" Nicky asked.

Ainsley nodded.

Nicky stared at her. "Just how many secrets are you keeping?"

Ainsley inhaled sharply, like those words had wounded her.

"Ms. Gibbons," she said, "do you know where Natalia is?"

"I swear to you," Ainsley said, "I do not know where she is. I haven't seen her in twenty years, since she was an infant."

"Then why were you so upset when we told you she was missing?" Nicky asked.

Ainsley looked right into her. Her cold, blue eyes seemed to be about to tear up. "I'm scared for her. I'm frightened for the first time in my life."

"You're lying," Nicky said, crossing her arms.

Ainsley opened her mouth, but Nicky didn't let her speak.

"You're gonna tell me where she is, or I'm telling Agent Walker to turn this place upside down until he finds whatever he's looking for."

Ainsley shook her head. "I'm not hiding anything. He's not going to find anything."

"Where are Marissa and James, Ainsley?" Nicky pressed.

She puffed up, her nostrils flaring. "I said leave my children out of this."

At that moment, Nicky's hunch turned into a full-blown epiphany.

Ainsley was protecting her children.

Nicky was about to press more when she heard Ken call from upstairs: "Upstairs is clear!"

She turned to call back—just as something cold and hard smashed into the back of her head.

She fell to her knees, her cheek crushed against the hardwood floor. She tried to shake the cobwebs out of her head and roll over, but she couldn't move. She heard Ainsley's footsteps behind her, running out the front door, as her vision faded to black.

CHAPTER EIGHTEEN

Nicky's eyes fluttered open to a feeling of warmth around her, and a smell, like sea and cologne...

Something was wrapped around her. No, not something—someone. Above her, Ken's face came into focus. His mouth was moving, but she couldn't hear his words. He gently tapped her face, and she snapped up as remembrance hit her.

"Lyons, are you—"

"She ran!" Nicky yelled, shooting upright. She'd been resting on Ken's lap, and he let her go as she pulled herself up. "We have to get her," she said, but then all the blood rushed to her head. She clutched at the back of her head, and it throbbed in protest.

"Hey, take it easy," Ken said. "She hit you good, Lyons. You could have a concussion."

Nicky looked beside them. On the tile floor, a massive brass candle holder was lying there. Nicky could only assume this was the weapon Ainsley had used to bash her in the back of the head. It still hurt like hell, but she was lucky she wasn't dead. Even a small woman could kill somebody with a weapon as heavy as that, which explained the still-pounding pain at the back of her skull.

"Lyons," Ken said, taking her hand, "you should lie down."

"I'm fine," she said, shaking him off. She looked around, trying to get her bearings. They were in the front hallway. A large, overstuffed couch was down the hall in the living room, and the door she came in was on her right, along with the staircase. She looked up and saw stairs leading to the second floor, then back to the front door, which was left wide open, letting the warm nighttime air into the house.

Still delirious, Nicky tried to stand. Ken stood with her, holding his hands on her to keep her up. She felt like shit, but she didn't have time to waste worrying about that.

"We have to catch Ainsley," she said. "She ran out there, into the woods. Ken, we have to go after her."

Ken hesitated. "Lyons, look at you. You're going to go out there and get yourself killed. She hit you hard in the head, you—"

"What the hell do you mean?" Nicky demanded. "I'm fine, Walker, now let's go!" She went to run away, but her head became woozy. She felt Ken gently grab her arm.

"Nicky, come on...I don't want..."

She met his eyes firmly. She could see in them, in that moment, that he just didn't want her to get hurt. But Nicky didn't care about anything else right now. Her head felt like it was being cleaved in half, but she had to catch Ainsley. She had to find Natalia.

"We can't waste any more time," she said, ripping her arm away from Ken. With that, she jogged out of the house and into the night, ignoring the pain. Ken sighed behind her and ran after.

"Okay, but I already called backup," he said. "They'll be here any second. We've got choppers coming. We'll get her."

"I can't just sit here," Nicky told him. "I'm going after her."

She faced the woods that stretched long and dark before them. Ainsley's footprints were in the dirt. But Nicky was an FBI agent. She could handle this. She could track down one woman.

But her head was still throbbing. She took deep breaths, trying to get the world to stop spinning.

"Lyons, are you sure you should be—"

"Just trust me, Walker," Nicky said, even though she loved him for his concern.

He stopped and looked up at the sky. "I can't believe I'm saying this, but maybe you should sit this one out, Nicky."

"What?" Nicky asked, but then she saw it too. Flashing lights in the sky, red and blue. More helicopters, coming in fast. She looked behind her, then back at the tree line. Ainsley had to be hiding in there. They'd find her somewhere.

But the choppers were getting closer.

"We've got backup coming," Ken said. "You should sit this out."

But Nicky didn't want to. She felt like she was on the brink of something really big, like this was it—the missing piece to this whole thing.

She had to find Ainsley.

"I'm going," she said firmly.

"Nicky—"

Nicky didn't waste any more time. She darted into the woods after Ainsley, the sticks cracking like bones beneath her feet as she ran into the darkness.

"Lyons, wait—"

But she didn't listen to Ken's warning. She just ran, following the trail of broken sticks and leaves behind Ainsley. She ran as fast as she could, even as her body protested.

Running through the darkness, running through the trees...it all brought her back to that night.

That night she'd escaped her and Rosie's kidnapper. That night she'd ran through the woods, leaving Rosie behind.

Nicky knew it was insane. That she was delirious. Maybe even dreaming. But in a way, by saving Natalia, she felt like she'd be saving Rosie too. It was all part of her redemption.

That was why she couldn't—wouldn't—give up.

All those years ago, Nicky had abandoned her sister. It still haunted her to this day. Everything she did was to make up for leaving Rosie behind.

As she ran, she remembered something Rosie had said to her years ago, before they were kidnapped, when Nicky was only fourteen and Rosie was thirteen. It was an odd question that had seemed to come out of nowhere.

"What happens if I get kidnapped?" she'd asked Nicky.

Nicky had just rolled her eyes. "That's just something that happens in movies, Ro. It's not real."

"What if we do get kidnapped?"

"Then I'll save you," Nicky had said, sounding so confident. "I'll always save you."

"Yeah," Rosie had said.

"You know what I wish?" Rosie had asked.

Nicky paused to think. "What?"

"I wish we were superheroes," Rosie said, her eyes bright. "I would be Supergirl."

"I would be Wonder Woman." Nicky said. "The real Wonder Woman."

Rosie had looked at her, annoyed. "Really?" she asked, incredulously. "Why?"

"Because," said Nicky, "I have it on good authority that Wonder Woman has the best outfit."

It was those small moments that Nicky held onto. The ones that were lighthearted; the ones where things were normal.

Still, Nicky couldn't help but wonder—why had Rosie asked the question about kidnapping, then superheroes? Maybe it was just because she'd seen a superhero movie where a person got kidnapped. But it all felt eerie to think of now.

Nicky had failed Rosie back then, but she wouldn't fail her now. She wasn't going to fail anyone anymore.

And as she ran through the woods, in the dead of night, following Ainsley's footprints, she felt like she was finally doing something right.

Why had Ainsley done it? Why had she taken the girl? She clearly had a motive.

The helicopters were right on top of her. She fell to her knees as the bright lights blinded her, momentarily blowing out her vision. She covered her face and waited for them to pass.

The helicopters hovered over the trees, their searchlights penetrating every part of the forest. After a moment, they moved on, flying away.

Nicky got up, feeling like she could vomit. Her head was still pounding. She wished she could just lie down and sleep for the next day. But she had to keep going. She had to find Ainsley.

She had to find Natalia.

These damn helicopters were going to tip Ainsley off, but maybe that would work in Nicky's favor. She might be trying to run from the choppers—she might not be expecting to be ambushed on foot.

Ken was somewhere behind her, running through the trees. Nicky got up and kept moving, dodging bushes and stepping over overturned logs. She still had Ainsley's trail—she could see the way the sticks had been shoved away as Ainsley had made her way through here.

Nicky was lucky that she was still conscious—that she was still on her feet by force of will, running blind with the help of the forest around her. But as she ran, she tripped on a tree root and fell hard on her knees. She stumbled to her feet, ignoring the pain in her leg.

She could feel a drop of blood drip off her chin. She must have bit her lip. She was sweating and breathing hard. She had to catch Ainsley.

"Lyons!" Ken called after her.

Nicky ran faster.

She'd been a track star in high school. She was a damn good runner. She could do this.

She ran even faster, her lungs burning like hell, her leg throbbing.

Ainsley had a decent head start, but Nicky was determined to catch her. She had to.

A flash of lightning cut across the sky and illuminated the forest. She felt the adrenaline in her veins, her heart pounding.

Ainsley's footsteps were getting harder to follow. Nicky was getting tired, and she was running out of trail. She had to find some kind of clue—some kind of sign.

As if on cue, a helicopter flew ahead in the distance, and Nicky heard a gasp in the woods.

A gasp that didn't come from her.

She kept running toward the sound of the noise. She broke through to a clearing in the forest, and that was when she saw her—Ainsley, crouching behind a tree, sobbing and clutching her head in her hands.

"Ainsley," Nicky said, trying to catch her breath. "Ainsley, stop running. It's over."

Ainsley turned around, her face a mess of tears.

"I can't do it anymore," she said. "I can't do it."

Nicky frowned. "Do what? Did you hurt Natalia?"

Ainsley shook her head. "No, I didn't. I didn't."

She broke into more hysterical sobs, just as Ken ran into the clearing. "Nicky—" he started, but stopped when he saw Ainsley, collapsed on the ground. The helicopters were still flying overhead, searching.

The pain at the back of Nicky's head struck her again. She clutched at her skull and touched the back, then she saw it: blood on her fingers.

Ken ran up to her. "Lyons, it's worse than I thought, you need—"

But Nicky felt herself getting woozy again.

She looked at the blood on her fingers. This wasn't a dream. It was all real.

"Nicky!"

She stumbled back, her vision going dark. "No," she mumbled as she collapsed in the forest.

CHAPTER NINETEEN

Nicky slowly opened her eyes and tried to focus on the nearby lights. White sheets, a pale light above her. She was in a hospital bed. She slowly tried to sit up but felt disoriented and nauseous. A nurse, who had been writing on a clipboard at the foot of the bed, quickly came over and helped her lie down.

"What happened?" Nicky asked.

"You hit your head pretty hard," the nurse said, putting a hand on Nicky's shoulder to keep her from sitting up again. "You have a concussion, so stay still."

Nicky winced. That explained her pounding headache. She turned her eyes to the nearby window, watching the night sky. It was still dark.

"How long have I been out?" Nicky asked. "Where's my partner?"

"You just arrived an hour ago, ma'am," the nurse said. "You have a man waiting for you outside, but first, we have to check your vitals."

Nicky let out a breath. Thank God. It was still the same night. Not that much time had passed.

The nurse peered into Nicky's eyes and moved the light back and forth. Then she checked Nicky's reflexes, lifted her eyelids, and put a hand on either side of her face. "You definitely have a minor concussion," the nurse said, "but I think you're going to be okay."

"Good," Nicky said. "Because I need to get out of here. Now."

"I don't think—"

Just then, the door burst open, and Ken rushed in. "She's awake?" he asked, but before the nurse could answer, he was at her side. Nicky took momentary comfort in his presence at the side of her hospital bed.

"Lyons," he said, looking relieved. "Thank God. I was starting to worry."

"What happened?" Nicky asked.

"You lost a lot of blood. Turns out Ainsley whacked you harder than we realized."

Nicky touched the back of her head gingerly, wincing when her fingers brushed a particularly tender spot.

"Ainsley?" Nicky asked. "Did we catch her?"

Ken nodded. "She's in custody. She's not going anywhere."

Nicky let out a breath she didn't know she was holding and closed her eyes, sinking back into the pillows. It was over. Ainsley was caught.

"Did you talk to her yet?"

"I tried, but she wouldn't budge," Ken said. "She's back at the local precinct now. They're holding her until we can get there and interrogate her. We still have no idea where Natalia is."

The nurse, who was still standing there, said, "I'll go get the doctor, but Ms. Lyons—you should probably stay here for a while longer."

"I can't do that," Nicky said, already trying to get out of the bed. But her head pounded, and she leaned back.

"We'll get you some painkillers," the nurse said, smiling sympathetically, then left the room. Silence surrounded Nicky and Ken. He stared at her for a moment too long, and Nicky turned away, staring off at the wall, unsure what to say.

"What the hell happened back there?" Ken asked, cutting the silence. "I felt like I lost you."

Nicky couldn't bring herself to meet his eyes. Her memory of chasing Ainsley through the woods was hazy, but she knew she wasn't being herself.

"I just...I had to catch her," Nicky said. "In a weird way, I felt like I was doing it for Rosie. To redeem myself."

"You were thinking of your sister?" Ken asked.

Nicky nodded, emotion welling up inside her. "I always am."

Ken sighed, then sat down on the edge of the bed. "Lyons...I'm sorry about your sister. But you can't keep blaming yourself for what happened. It wasn't your fault."

Nicky's eyes started to water. She blinked hard. "I know that. But I just feel guilty, you know? If I wasn't such a screw-up, if I—"

"You're not a screw-up," Ken said. "You put your heart in every case. I see that now. Honestly, you know I was wary about letting someone younger and less experienced than me lead the team, but you have a drive like I've never seen before, Lyons. But you can be reckless, too, and that shows when you throw yourself into situations where you could get seriously hurt. I was—" He stopped himself, voice thick with emotion. But he held it all in and forced a small smile. Nicky couldn't ignore the feeling—the pull—inside her chest that was telling her to get closer to him. She'd never felt this way before.

"—I was worried," he finished.

Nicky looked away. "I'm sorry," she said.

But Ken reached over, put a hand on her shoulder, and drew her close; their faces were inches apart. "If anything happened to you, I don't know what I'd do," Ken said. "I don't think I could handle the team without you."

Nicky's chest tightened, and she felt herself leaning in closer to him. "You'd do fine," she whispered, feeling breathless.

Ken's eyes seemed to be searching hers. "Nicky," he whispered, moving in even closer to her, "I know this isn't the right time...And I know I haven't been the most open—"

He was interrupted by the sudden opening of the door. The doctor was there. "Ms. Lyons?" the doctor asked, glancing from Ken to Nicky and back. "I was told you were awake."

"Uh, yeah, that's me," she replied, wishing he hadn't come in.

"I've got your pain medication here. I assume you want some?"

Nicky nodded.

"I'll give it a moment to kick in, then you can leave." He turned to Ken. "I'm afraid you'll have to wait outside until I'm done examining Ms. Lyons."

"Of course," Ken said. He gave Nicky an embarrassed look and left.

"You're in good hands, Ms. Lyons," the doctor said, as Nicky's head began to swirl with dizziness. He put the pill in her hand and helped her swallow it.

"Thanks," Nicky said. "How bad is it?"

"We did an MRI on you while you were sleeping, and there's no permanent damage," the doctor explained. "But you definitely need rest."

"I can't rest," Nicky said. "I'm working a case that's more important than anything else right now."

"I understand," the doctor said. "But please—you need to take care of yourself too. You're not a help to anyone if you get too hurt. Please, be careful."

If only this doctor knew her—he'd know she wouldn't rest until Natalia was home and safe. She needed to get down to the precinct and talk to Ainsley. But she nodded, saying, "Thanks, Doc. I will."

Once the doctor was gone, Nicky headed for the door, but the room started spinning. She got dizzy just trying to reach the doorknob. But she managed to open the door and walked out.

Ken was leaning against the wall, holding his phone to his ear, but he saw her and immediately hung up. "Lyons—"

"I'm fine," Nicky said. "The doctor said I just need some rest. Let's go."

"All right," Ken said. "But this time, I'm driving."

CHAPTER TWENTY

At the local precinct, Nicky stared down Ainsley Gibbons's cold, blue eyes across from her in the interrogation room. Her head still hurt, but the painkillers had kicked in, and she felt safe with Ken beside her in the room.

"You really did a number on me, Ms. Gibbons," Nicky said. She couldn't help but feel anger and resentment toward this woman who had ruthlessly hit her over the head with something that could have killed her, and she'd be sure that Ainsley saw adequate charges for that.

But first, she needed to know where the hell Natalia Cavazos was. She was done messing around.

Ainsley merely looked away, her expression stoic and cold.

"Hey," Ken cut in, his voice stern, "you could have killed her. You know that, right?" He sounded more pissed than Nicky was.

Ainsley looked at him. "Maybe."

"I don't think you understand what you've done here," Nicky said, leaning closer to Ainsley, who glared at her. "You've committed a crime against a federal agent, and you're being investigated for kidnapping the vice president's daughter. You're looking at a long time in prison, Ms. Gibbons."

"I don't care," Ainsley said, and there was something in her voice—a weariness, maybe—that caught Nicky off guard.

"You don't care?" Nicky asked. "You don't care that your children will lose their mother? You don't care that your nice, cushy life will be gone forever?"

A look of resentment flashed across Ainsley's face, but she quickly suppressed it. "I don't care," she said. "I'm not the one who kidnapped the girl."

"Then who did?" Nicky asked.

Ainsley bit her lip.

"Was it one of your children?"

"How dare you talk to me about my children?" Ainsley asked, her voice hard and bitter.

"I'm just saying—"

"You know nothing about me," Ainsley said. "For all you know, I'm an amazing mother. And my kids don't even like me."

"Wait, what?" Nicky asked, taken aback. "Why?"

Ainsley sighed, looking down. "Because no one likes me," she said. "I'm...I'm a horrible person."

"We're not here to judge you," Ken said. He seemed truly sympathetic.

Ainsley laughed, a hard, bitter laugh. "I'm a liar and a cheat," she snapped. "I'm a bad mother and a bad friend. I'm...I'm a bad person, alright?"

Nicky felt herself growing uncomfortable. She wasn't good at this sort of thing, the whole "pity the criminal" thing.

"Ainsley," Nicky said, "we're just trying to find out where Natalia is." She was done with Ainsley's cold, callous gaze. "Where did you take her?"

Ainsley didn't say a word.

"Ainsley—" Nicky said, a hint of warning in her voice, but Ainsley still didn't answer.

"You should talk to her," Ken said. He knelt down beside her chair and glared into Ainsley's eyes. "We know you care more than you're letting on."

Ainsley's eyes flickered with surprise, but then she shook her head. "Fine. You want the truth? I don't give a shit about Natalia. Steven has two other children who deserve his time, yet he gave it all to that girl."

"That girl is his daughter," Nicky said. Ainsley wasn't doing herself any favors. She sounded bitter, resentful, and spiteful. All motivations to do something terrible to Natalia. "What has she ever done to you?" Nicky asked.

"He never noticed our children," Ainsley said. Her eyes looked up at the ceiling with a mixture of loathing and longing. "He never noticed us, never recognized us as his real family. But Natalia? He'd make time for her. He'd take her to dinner and give her presents. He'd spend hours with her, listening to her talk about her day, her life. It was sickening. Who cares about that little girl? He was supposed to be with me. He wasn't supposed to care about her."

"And so you kidnapped her?" Nicky asked, feeling nauseous. Her head felt like it was splitting open. She wanted to hit Ainsley. She wanted to make her suffer. But she still needed to know where Natalia was. "You've put her life in danger."

"No," Ainsley said. "No, I didn't. I...I want to talk to Steven."

"Steven doesn't know you're here," Nicky said, which was true—if she let the VP know that they had Ainsley in custody, then she feared he'd come down and try to intervene. They needed total control of this case. "And he's not going to know," she added. "Is that why you're doing all this? To get the vice president's attention? To get Steven's attention?"

"Yes," Ainsley said, glaring at Nicky. "Isn't that sick enough for you?" She leaned back in her chair. "Steven Cavazos is a sorry excuse for a father. He neglected Marissa. He neglected James. He neglected me...all for a fake life with that other family of his."

"You should have told him how you felt," Ken said. "Not kidnapped his daughter."

"I did tell him," Ainsley said, her eyes falling to the table. "He didn't listen. He didn't care." She lifted her eyes back to Nicky.

"So you wanted to punish him," Nicky said.

"He'd deserve it," Ainsley said. "He was never a father to our children. He just paid the bills. It was never enough. He should have been with me."

Ainsley was twenty years younger than Steven—maybe that was why their relationship had been doomed from the start. Maybe Steven had never intended to stay with her. Maybe Ainsley was just being naïve.

"Steven was a married man," Nicky reminded her. "He was taken."

"Shut up!" Ainsley snapped at her. "I told him to leave her. I told him he had to choose me. He didn't listen. He was never going to listen. He was with her. He was always with her."

"You kidnapped Natalia," Nicky said, trying to keep her voice steady. "You're guilty of that."

"I didn't kidnap her," Ainsley said, calm and collected. "And I didn't hurt her. I'm not a monster. I'm not."

"You're going to need witnesses to attest to that. You know where she is," Nicky said through gritted teeth.

"I don't have her."

A knock at the door cut them off, and a panicked-looking officer poked his head in. "Agent Lyons, the...the secret service is here."

Shit. Nicky could not have them meddling with this—not when she was so close. "Walker, go distract them," Nicky said. The feet of Ken's chair scraped against the floor as he stood, and he dashed out of the room with the other cop, letting the door shut behind them.

The pressure was on now. No more messing around.

Nicky met Ainsley's eyes firmly. There was one thing Nicky hadn't been focusing on enough—and that was the dash on the side of Ainsley's face. It was clear that she'd been in a fight in her home before Nicky and Ken had arrived at her house earlier.

"Who did that, Ainsley?" Nicky pressed.

"Nobody," she replied. "I fell."

"That's not true."

Nicky thought back to earlier, the thought she'd had—that Ainsley was protecting her children. They still hadn't located Marissa and James.

So far, nothing had seemed to work to truly get Ainsley to crack. Steven was a trigger, but her children...

"Was it one of your children, Ainsley?" Nicky asked, and Ainsley's nostrils flared.

"Excuse me?"

"Did one of your children hit you? Maybe the girl? Maybe Marissa?"

"How dare you," Ainsley said.

Her voice was icy, but her face was flushed, and Nicky knew that she'd hit a nerve. Ainsley was hiding something, and the only way to get to that something was to get her angry.

"Marissa could hurt you, Ainsley," Nicky continued. "She's a young woman. She could overpower you and hurt you. Hurt you so bad that you'd never get up again."

"Shut up."

"She could kill you, couldn't she? That's why you have to protect her, isn't it? Because she can hurt you. Because you're afraid of what she might do. Because you know she could—"

Ainsley stood up and threw the chair across the room, hitting the wall with a crash. "Shut up!" she screamed.

Nicky didn't stop. "That's why you're protecting her, isn't it? Tell me where your children are, Ainsley, or I'll make sure all of you go to jail for a long time."

Ainsley's glare was murderous. "I'm not saying anything else without Steven," she said. "I want to talk to him."

"You'll never see him again," Nicky said. "I'll personally make sure of that."

A look of pure rage flashed across Ainsley's face, and that was when Nicky knew that she'd struck the final chord.

Ainsley dove across the table and lunged right at Nicky.

CHAPTER TWENTY ONE

This time, Nicky was prepared for Ainsley's attack. She bent at the waist and swooped a leg behind Ainsley's knees. The women's legs collided with each other, and Ainsley went crashing to the floor. A rush of dizziness hit Nicky, but she pushed through. Nicky leapt on top of her, pinning her arms at her sides.

"Stay down, don't move," Nicky hissed in Ainsley's ear. Ainsley struggled against her, but Nicky was too strong. She was a trained agent, and Ainsley was a frail woman.

"Where is she?" Nicky asked. "Where is Natalia Cavazos?"

"I'm not talking to you anymore!" Ainsley screamed.

"Tell me where she is!" Nicky repeated, still pinning Ainsley to the floor.

Ainsley didn't give her an answer. Nicky sighed and stood up, leaving her face to the floor. Ainsley was a bitter, resentful, and pathetic woman. Nicky needed to make her talk, but she was running out of ideas—and patience. She grabbed Ainsley by her elbow and shoved her back onto the chair, blowing a strand of sweaty hair off her face as she sat down across from her, as if that assault had never happened. Ainsley's cold blue eyes locked on Nicky's, more deranged than ever.

"Tell me where your children are," Nicky said.

"I'm not telling you anything," Ainsley said, her voice a low hiss. "You're going to have to find them yourself. You're going to have to work for it, Agent Lyons. You're going to have to work hard."

"Fine," Nicky said, shoving the chair back and standing up. "I'll do what I have to. Believe me when I say this—finding your kids is the least of your problems."

She had a feeling she'd have to if she wanted to get Ainsley to talk, but she really wasn't sure that she did. Above all, Nicky wanted Natalia found. If that meant Ainsley had to suffer, then Nicky would suffer with her.

She didn't have to go far to start making things happen. She'd already gotten into Ainsley's head—now, she just had to get her to confess.

Just as Nicky was about to throw more words Ainsley's way, the door flew open, and in strode the vice president of the United States.

At that moment, Ainsley cracked. She looked at Steven, and he looked at her. The tension was thick and palpable, Nicky could cut it with a knife.

She stood up. "Sir—"

Ken and two secret service agents came in behind the VP. Steven looked at Ainsley with fury in his eyes.

"What did you do to my daughter?"

Ainsley choked up. "I didn't, I—"

"Bullshit," Steven hissed. "Where the hell is Natalia?"

Ainsley didn't say anything. She couldn't.

"Where is my daughter?" Steven asked.

Ainsley looked up at him, her eyes glistening with tears. "I don't know."

"Agent Lyons," Steven said, turning to her. "What is she talking about?"

"I don't know, Sir," Nicky said. "I don't know where Natalia is. She isn't talking. Right now, I'm trying to figure out where Marissa and James are."

"I said to leave them out of this," Ainsley snapped.

The VP had his eyes locked on Ainsley still. "Where are they, Ainsley?"

But she didn't speak, just looked away. Nicky sighed and walked over to the VP. The more she could learn about Ainsley—about Marissa and James—the better she could get this information out of the woman. Nicky left the interrogation room, and the two secret service agents followed behind—but Nicky looked at them and said, "I need to talk to the VP alone."

"Sir—" one of the agents started, but the VP held up a hand.

"It's fine. Leave us."

Nicky locked eyes with Ken once more and nodded before leaving him and the two secret service agents alone with Ainsley in the room. In the hallway, alone, Nicky faced the vice president.

"You should have called me as soon as you took her in," the VP said.

"I was in the hospital," Nicky told him. "Your mistress in there whacked me over the back of the head with a brass candlestick."

Emotion flickered over Steven's face. "I'm sorry, Agent Lyons. That's terrible. Are you okay?"

"I'm fine, Sir," she said. "But we wanted to talk to Ainsley alone and try to get information out of her. I'm sorry we didn't call you."

"Well, it's fine...but has she said anything?"

"No, Sir, but I get the sense that Marissa and James might know something. Ainsley won't tell me where they are." Nicky paused, gauging the VP's reaction. A flicker of guilt flashed across his face. "Sir," Nicky said. "You don't know them very well, do you, even though they're your children too?"

The VP sighed. "You're right. I barely know them at all."

He paused. "I've been too busy."

"So they must be angry at you," she said. She was fishing, but she was hoping to find some sort of clue in the VP's reactions. "Think they'd want to...get back to you?"

"I didn't think Marissa and James even knew I was their father," he said. "Maybe Ainsley told them..."

"They didn't know?" Nicky asked.

"I have so much shame, Agent Lyons." The VP turned away from her. "I hated her so much," he said. "I hated Ainsley. She did this to me. She did this to my family." He looked back at Nicky. "Do you have any idea what it's like to have your own life ruined by someone you loved?"

"I don't," Nicky said quietly. "I'm sorry."

"I never thought Ainsley would do something like this," he said. "But in the end, it's all my fault. I thought I could throw money at her and the kids, and that they would just leave me alone if I kept a roof over their heads."

Nicky was stunned. She'd heard Steven speak before, but she'd never seen him speak so candidly—so vulnerably, even. She didn't know what to say to that, so she just stood there, not saying anything.

Steven shook his head. "But I never did anything, did I? I never even tried."

Nicky stayed silent.

"What she did to my family is unforgivable," Steven said. "I don't know how I'm going to forgive her."

Nicky hesitated a second, but then she said, "With time."

He looked at her, and she could see the years of bitterness and sorrow in his eyes.

"I wish I could be there for my kids," Steven said. "But I can't. I can't do that to the country."

“They’re your children,” Nicky said, the confidence and power rising in her voice. “You don’t have to choose between them and the country. They can figure things out. And they’re both adults, they can make their own decisions, they can—”

“Ainsley is their mother,” Steven interrupted. “That trumps everything. I can’t let Marissa and James throw their lives away on a woman who could do that to me.”

“Ainsley is their mother,” Nicky agreed. “But you’re their father. Maybe they didn’t do anything to Natalia. Maybe this is all on Ainsley. Maybe it’s not too late for them.”

Even as Nicky was saying it, she didn’t fully believe it. Ainsley was definitely protecting her kids, and with Marissa and James nowhere to be found, they were looking more and more guilty.

If they just recently found out that Natalia Cavazos is their half-sister, and Steven Cavazos is their father...then maybe they snapped.

Nicky wasn’t sure. But the only one who had the answers was in that interrogation room. She had to get Ainsley to talk.

She was grateful to see that she had gained his trust, but it was time to get back to Ainsley and see if she could get the information Nicky needed to find Natalia.

Nicky returned to the interrogation room alone, leaving the vice president behind. The two secret service agents looked at her as she entered the room, and she gave them a single nod. They nodded back and left the room.

She was glad they had backed off. She didn’t want them interfering with her questioning. Ken sat wordlessly at the interrogation table across from Ainsley. Nicky crossed to the interrogation table and put her hands on the table, on either side of Ainsley.

Ainsley looked up at Nicky. “I’m sorry,” she whispered. “I’m so sorry.”

“What are you sorry for?” Nicky asked.

“For...for hurting Steven.”

Nicky sat down and exchanged a look with Ken. Maybe the stress was finally getting to her.

“Are you ready to confess?” Nicky asked.

Ainsley looked at Nicky with bleary, blue eyes and sighed. “Yes. Yes, I am.”

CHAPTER TWENTY TWO

Nicky's heart stalled. Was Ainsley really ready to confess? She held her breath as she faced the woman down in the interrogation room, hoping—praying—that this was it. Natalia Cavazos could be returned safely to her father.

This could all be over.

"But you have to promise me something," Ainsley said.

Nicky hesitated. "What do you want?"

"You...you can't hurt them," she said. "You can't hurt my children."

Nicky took a second to think. Could she give this woman a promise like that? "I promise I'll do everything I can to make sure your children are not hurt."

"Thank you," Ainsley said. "Thank you so much. You have no idea what this means..."

Nicky took a deep breath. She had to focus. She couldn't get caught up in the weirdness of the moment. She had to focus.

Ainsley began to talk.

"I...I didn't want—" Ainsley's eyes glazed over, and she shook her head.

"—I'm sorry," she said. "They...they didn't do anything."

"Ainsley, what did you do?" Nicky asked.

"I...I didn't want to hurt him," she said. "I love him."

"Who?"

"Steven. I love him." Ainsley let out a sob. "I...I didn't want to hurt him. But I did. I hurt him..."

"What did you do?" Nicky asked.

"All those years ago, Steven made me a promise," Ainsley said. "He promised that he'd make sure myself and my children would be taken care of forever. But he also made me promise that I could never tell them the truth. Marissa and James...they could never know who their real father was. They could never know that Steven Cavazos was their father.

"But then, I found out he was going to cut my benefits. He was going to throw me out into the streets. He was going to destroy my family." Her face was twisted into an ugly picture of hatred.

Wait...what? The vice president had not, at all, mentioned that he was going to cut Ainsley off. Ainsley could be lying, but Nicky's instant gut feeling was that this whole thing smelled off—and that the vice president's hands weren't clean either. In this case, Nicky believed Ainsley was telling the truth.

Nicky's fists clenched. She felt like she'd been played. Then again, leave it to a politician to lie and try to absolve all guilt.

"Did he give a reason why?" Nicky asked.

"Yes," she said. "He mentioned that his wife had noticed the money being transferred to unknown accounts, which were mine. He feared she was close to finding out about me."

Nicky's nails dug into her palms. It all seemed so scummy. As a federal agent, of course she respected the vice president of the United States, but as a woman, she had to admit, this was all terrible.

For a moment, she found herself empathizing with Ainsley. As a young woman, she'd been swept into an illustrious affair with a powerful politician. He'd left her pregnant, refused to partake in her children's lives, and now, all these years later, he was threatening to break the only vow he ever truly made to her.

"When I found that out," Ainsley said, "I was devastated. I became a single mother, raising Steven's kids without him, and the only support I've had has been from him for the last twenty years...then he said he was going to cut me off. He was going to throw me out into the street. He made me promise that I wouldn't tell the kids who their father was, and he was keeping his word. He was providing a way for me to live, so I had to keep my word too. Steven said it was the only way he could keep his word to me. When he told me he was cutting me off, I was angry, and so I told Marissa and James the truth."

Nicky's heart raced. "And then they kidnapped Natalia for revenge?"

"No," Ainsley said. Her eyes were full of shame now. "No...it was me who kidnapped Natalia. I was going to use her for leverage, hold her ransom, and make Steven promise to keep supporting me and my children. But when I took her to the house, Marissa and James, they...they wanted to do something more. They wanted to make Steven really pay."

Nicky looked at Ken, who wore the same worried expression.

The same expression of fear—fear that they were already too late to save Natalia.

"What happened to them?" Nicky asked.

"I...I don't know," Ainsley said. "Marissa knocked me out. When I woke up, Natalia and my children were gone. I was too afraid to leave the house. You showed up a couple hours later."

Nicky's head spun in circles. She was going to need to fill in the vice president on all of this.

"I'm so sorry," Ainsley said. "I never meant for this to happen. I never meant for my children to go to jail for their half-sister's murder. Please...you have to find them. We have a guest house. Maybe she's there. They also have a boat."

Nicky nodded. "I will find them. Thank you for your cooperation, Ainsley. We'll make sure you're processed comfortably."

Ainsley nodded, hanging her head low in shame. "I am sorry...Steven, I'm so sorry..."

Nicky and Ken stood. Ken had been quiet the whole time, and Nicky wondered what he was thinking about all of this.

They left to the hallway, where police officers were standing by. "Take care of her," Nicky told one of them, and the officer sped inside the interrogation room.

Ainsley had confessed to kidnapping. She'd assaulted a federal agent—twice. As much as Nicky did feel for her now, she knew Ainsley's best place was behind bars. Maybe they'd let her off easy and put her on house arrest, but it was out of Nicky's hands now.

Frankly, all she cared about was finding Natalia.

The vice president must have already left, because as Nicky and Ken made their way through the police station, there was no sign of the secret service anywhere. Ken had been very quiet, and they passed through to outside, met by the warm night. It was getting late now, after midnight, and the clock was ticking on this case.

"You okay?" she asked Ken as they found their way to the car.

He nodded. "I don't know how I feel about any of this."

"I'm not sure how I feel about it either," Nicky said. "But we to do our jobs. We have to find Natalia. She's in danger."

"You don't think..."

"What?"

"I don't think this woman could kidnap her witho said. "Could she have hired a professional? Someone to and then kill her? I just can't believe this woman would do something like this," Ken said.

"She and her children have a lot of problems," Nicky said. "This is how they express their issues...by kidnapping. It's a terrible thing, and I'm not trying to justify what they did, but it is how they work. They aren't 'sane' in the way that we would expect. And I think we have to remember that."

Nicky went for the driver's side, but Ken placed a gentle hand on her arm. She stopped, confused.

"You still have a concussion," Ken said. "Let me drive."

"I'm fine," Nicky said.

She hated being a passenger. It reminded her of all those years ago, when she and Rosie were kidnapped by that man—when he'd thrown them in the back of his van and drove them out to the woods. Nicky had been powerless back then, but she had taken control back now. Being the driver made her feel like she had that control.

And she did feel fine now. The painkillers had kicked in.

"I can drive, Ken," she said.

"Nicky, come on," he told her. "Just...let me care about you for once."

He was upset, and Nicky could see it in his face.

"Fine," she told him. "But I'm driving when we get to Ainsley's."

"Thank you," Ken said, and he opened the driver's side door for her.

Once Nicky was inside, Ken walked to the other side. His mood was tense, and Nicky didn't blame him—this case was a lot to handle.

Nicky started the engine. "Let's go. We have a guest house to check out."

CHAPTER TWENTY THREE

Natalia's feet slowly thumped over the dock, leading out onto the sea as turbulent waves spread before her. So close to the sea at night, she was freezing in her bikini—freezing and terrified for her life.

Something cold and hard jabbed her in the back.

She knew what it was.

A gun.

Her kidnappers prodded her forward, forcing her toward the edge of the dock. "Keep going," the girl said.

"Don't stop," the guy added.

"Who are you?" Natalia's voice shook as she walked. "Why do you hate me so much?"

She didn't understand who they were or why they'd kidnapped her. It didn't make any sense.

"I'm—I'm the vice president's daughter," she said. "He'll pay for me. I promise. Please, just let me go..."

She hated the way she sounded. Pathetic. Scared. Would they kill her?

"He'll pay. I promise," she repeated.

The kidnappers laughed.

"You're so stupid. You have no idea who we are, do you?" the girl said.

"I just wanna go home," Natalia pleaded.

"You are home," the guy said.

"What?" she asked, confused. Only a few steps left.

The girl laughed.

"You're home, stupid."

Her mouth began to tremble, and she tried to calm herself, but she was so afraid. They reached the edge of the dock, where a boat was docked, rocking in the waves.

"Get on," the girl said.

Natalia's feet stopped at the edge of the dock. She felt like if she got on that boat, it would be the last thing she ever did.

But they had a gun.

They could shoot her.

She had to listen.

She climbed on board. Natalia's chest tightened as she stepped onto the boat, her feet sinking into the wooden floor. The gun was still pointed at her as she took another step, then another, until she stepped up to the front of the boat, and the girl lowered it.

"Move."

The boat had two seats.

"Sit in the back," the guy said.

She did as she was told, sitting in the back of the boat, where the waves hit the hardest. The boat rocked, and the engine roared. A shot of adrenaline shot through her, and she knew they were leaving the shore.

"I'm going to pay you. I promise, I'll pay you," she said.

"Shut up."

Natalia bit her lip, shut her mouth, and hung her head. She'd be taken back to shore as soon as her dad paid. This would all be over, right? Surely, there had to be a way out of this.

Natalia's head spun with thoughts.

How had this happened?

How did she get here?

She didn't understand.

And her body was cold, too cold. The waves hit her body and it was freezing, but the kidnappers didn't seem to care. The boat moved away from the shore and into the sea, riding through the waves, picking up speed.

"How much do you want?" she asked.

Her dad would pay them. Even if they demanded so much that he had to sell the country, her dad would pay.

"Just shut up," the girl said.

Natalia sat in the seat, trembling and terrified. They were going to kill her.

The boat moved away from shore, with the guy piloting it. Natalia had to escape. Her fight or flight instincts activated. She couldn't just let them take her out to sea and kill her. She had to do something to get away.

The shore grew farther and farther away. She had to think fast. What could she do to save herself?

Swim, she told herself. *You have to jump. You have to swim.*

She had to.

Natalia took a deep breath in and closed her eyes.

She couldn't escape like this. She had to do something even if she died.

She'd jump and swim.

Natalia opened her eyes.

She threw herself forward and dove into the water, gulping mouthfuls as she went.

She couldn't look back.

She couldn't think of anything.

She had to fight.

As she swam away from the boat, her mind was on fire, and she didn't stop to think of what would happen next.

Maybe I'll die.

Maybe I'll get eaten by a shark.

Maybe I'll get away.

There wasn't time to think about it.

She just had to go.

And go she did. She swam as hard as she could, swimming away from the boat, then away from the shore.

She couldn't think about where she was swimming to, she just had to go.

She had to save herself.

Natalia's body pounded with adrenaline as she swam in the dark waters as far away from the boat as she could.

As her feet kicked and her arms swam at the sea, she caught her breath, gulped down water, then kept swimming.

Her mind raced, and she felt tears streaming down her face, but she couldn't think about it. She had to keep pushing forward.

Natalia swam and swam and swam.

It felt like forever.

But she was free.

She'd escaped.

Until her head bobbed above water, and she dared to look back—only to see that the boat was following her.

How had they found her? They were following her. Her legs kicked harder. She tried to swim away. She tried to go faster. But the boat moved closer, and faster, and soon she could smell the breath of the kidnappers.

"Bitch," the guy said.

Natalia swam some more, but he was right behind her.

She had to keep going.

She couldn't go back.

Natalia's body ached as she swam. Her arms ached, her legs ached, and her cheeks stung from the salty sea water, and she knew she wouldn't make it far before she collapsed.

She had to get away.

The boat moved closer and closer. The kidnappers laughed, but she kept swimming. She had no choice.

Hope washed away from her.

She couldn't do this.

She couldn't keep going.

Natalia's body burned as she swam, and she felt like she couldn't breathe through the burning ache in her lungs. She wanted to cry, but she didn't have time.

She pushed on, swimming away from the boat, until she was so tired, she couldn't lift her head up anymore.

She tried to keep going, but her body wouldn't let her.

Her heart pounded.

Her head pounded.

Her legs gave out beneath her.

She couldn't swim anymore.

She couldn't fight.

She couldn't go on.

But when Natalia heard the gun cock behind her, she took another huge breath in and tried to swim.

"Stop!" the girl yelled.

Natalia stopped swimming and turned around.

The girl had her gun pointed at Natalia's head, and the boat was upon her now.

The kidnappers grabbed Natalia and forced her onto the boat, laughing at her as she lay helpless on the deck.

But Natalia refused to give up.

She glared at them with fire in her eyes, refusing to let them win.

They may have taken her once, but they would never take her again.

Natalia was a fighter, and she would find a way to get free from these ruthless kidnappers and survive this nightmare once and for all.

She lunged at the gun, desperate to make it hers, but the guy hit her across the face with a heavy fist. Natalia fell to the deck, just as storm clouds grumbled in the sky.

A crack of lightning, and a bolt of electricity split the sky, lighting up the ocean with its terrifying glow.

Natalia was furious. She picked herself up, wiped away the blood that streamed from her nose, and charged at the gun once again.

She didn't care what happened. She couldn't go back. She couldn't die.

But that was when the guy grabbed her, wrapping his hands around her shoulders, and didn't let go. She tried to turn and say something, but the words were trapped in her throat. Her feet were still on the ground, but her arms were being restrained now, and the ropes around her wrists were impossibly tight. Her whole body was being wrenched backward, and she didn't know what was happening.

They had her tied up, so she couldn't run. She couldn't swim. She couldn't fight.

She was powerless once again.

Her assailants looked down at her with vicious smirks.

They had her right where they wanted her.

CHAPTER TWENTY FOUR

Nicky and Ken hurried up to the Gibbons' guest house—only to find the door had been left wide open, and all the lights were off inside.

What the hell?

Nicky frowned as she walked in, gun drawn. On the wall, there was a large picture of Steven Cavazos—a portrait.

Odd. If the kids didn't even know who their father was, Nicky wondered if they ever asked their mother why she kept pictures of him in the guest house.

Maybe this was Steven's private getaway home to be with Ainsley. After learning that he was willing to cut Ainsley off—and had withheld that information from the FBI—Nicky no longer trusted what the vice president had to say. Based on the way Ainsley had been acting, Nicky would guess that he didn't just send her money over the years.

He was probably still sleeping with her too.

But none of that mattered now. They needed to find Natalia.

"I'll check upstairs," Nicky said to Ken, who also had his gun drawn. "You take the basement."

He nodded, and both of them split up. Nicky crept through the house, her heart pounding in her chest. She didn't know what they were going to find, but she was ready for anything.

The place was immaculate—so clean it looked like no one had ever been here before. This place was owned by a wealthy man who probably had help maintaining his property; it didn't look like he lived here.

She crept upstairs, her feet creaking on the floorboards. She reached the upper level and began clearing the rooms. There was no sign of life in here at all.

The bedroom was vacant. No Natalia.

The bathroom was vacant. No Natalia.

The guest room was vacant. No Natalia.

The closets were all empty. No Natalia.

And Nicky's heart dropped.

Nicky didn't want to accept that Natalia could be gone. But if the kidnappers had already left with her, she wouldn't be here.

So where was Natalia?

Where did they take her?

Nicky's stomach twisted in knots, and she felt sick to her stomach.

She went back downstairs, just as Ken came upstairs, and they met on the main level.

"It's all clear down there," Ken said.

"Same with upstairs. She's not here."

Damn it. They were already gone. But where could they be? Then, it hit her—the boat. Ainsley had mentioned that they had one, and of course, there was the gas cap found at the beach.

"They must have taken the boat," Nicky said. "Maybe they had her here, then moved her."

Nicky felt like she was going to throw up. The kidnappers had Natalia. They could take her anywhere.

They could kill her anywhere.

But where would they go this late? Nicky's heart squeezed. The only person who really knew Marissa and James was Ainsley. Maybe she could get her on the phone to help. If they did take the boat, where would they go?

Nicky took out her phone and dialed the local precinct. Within a few rings, she connected to an officer. "This is Agent Lyons," Nicky said. "Is Ainsley Gibbons still in custody?"

"She is," the officer said.

"I need to talk to her. Now."

"Hold on."

Nicky was placed on hold. She tapped her foot impatiently, willing the process to move faster. She watched the phone, waiting for the call to come through.

"H…hello?" a voice said.

"Ainsley," Nicky said. "It's Agent Lyons. Quickly, I need to ask you something. If your children took Natalia on the boat, where would they go?"

A long pause hung in the air. "I...well..."

"Please," Nicky said. "Ainsley. They will get caught. You can't protect them anymore. Help us...help Steven. Help Natalia. She's innocent in all this."

"I...I can't say for sure," Ainsley said. "There...there is an island off the coast where we would sometimes boat over. No one lives there. We would take vacations there, just us three...I remember sometimes, when we'd be up there, Marissa and James...they would talk about how they wished they had a father to be there with them."

Nicky paused. She had to admit that it struck a chord. There were so many times in her own life when she wished her own father was more present or was a different man entirely. So many experiences she had without a dad...

That had been Marissa and James's whole life.

"A…and where is this island?" Nicky said.

Ainsley took a deep breath. "It's about two hundred miles off the coast with the current. I can't remember the name. But it's been years since we were there. It hasn't been maintained."

"Damn it," Nicky said.

"They could be there now," Ainsley said. "There's a dock there if I recall. Maybe they brought Natalia there."

"Okay," Nicky said. "We'll look."

"Just...get my children," Ainsley said. "Get them before they do something that they can't come back from."

She hung up the phone. Nicky's heart crushed. "Okay," she said to Ken. "We know where they are. There's an island offshore, and Ainsley thinks they could be there."

She took off out the door. "Come on."

"Got it." Ken nodded. "I'll see if I can get the Coast Guard on the line."

Nicky nodded and backed up, her gun still drawn. "We need a helicopter too. They could be at sea. There are docks not far from here."

Nicky was ready to get going. She was ready to get to Natalia.

***

Nicky jogged through the woods with Ken at her side until they got down to the beach, where there was a large private dock. The rapids were rough, and the sound of crashing waves filled Nicky's ears. The moon shone through the stormy clouds above.

A helicopter waited down at the shore, and in it were two familiar faces: Danny and Rachel, the pilots Nicky and Ken had just dealt with the other day when dealing with the Clara Jones case. Nicky and Ken ran toward the helicopter.

Nicky was relieved to see them, but she also wanted to get going. "Danny, Rachel, it's good to see you again," Nicky said as she and Ken slipped into the back of the helicopter. They got strapped in. Nicky looked out over the helicopter, clicking the buckles into place.

"Agent Lyons, Agent Walker," Danny said. "We're here to help."

"Good," Nicky said. She was all strapped in. "We're looking for a boat. It should be heading toward a small island off the coast."

Nicky felt the familiar weight in her stomach as the helicopter lifted off into the air. The engine noise grew louder as they rose higher, and Nicky was filled with feelings of relief and apprehension. She reminded herself that she had been to this place before and she could do it again. She had a great team behind her, and she wouldn't have chosen anyone else to help her find Natalia.

They ascended into the windy nighttime air. Nicky leaned forward and scanned the waves for a sign of the boat. She didn't know how far the kidnappers had gotten, but she hoped she would know the boat when she saw it. She had no idea what boat they would be using, after all.

"Do you see anything?" Nicky asked.

Danny shook his head. "No, ma'am. Should we maybe go a little farther out?"

"Yes," Nicky said. "We're looking for a boat—it could still be at sea, or it could be at the island."

The pilots flew them farther over the turbulent sea.

"Wait," Ken said. "I see something."

"Where?" Nicky said, leaning forward. "I don't see anything."

"It's that way," Ken said. "I think."

Nicky shifted slightly in her seat. She saw it too, now. It was a boat—a dark, short boat. It was hard to tell from this distance, but it looked like it was coming toward the island, which Nicky could barely see in the darkness.

Nicky scanned the boat, looking for something—anything—that would tell her that Natalia was there. She had to find her.

The boat went right toward the island. But as soon as it was within a few hundred yards of the island, it veered away and headed out into the open sea.

"Damn it," Nicky said.

She leaned forward, pressing her eyes to the night vision binoculars. She watched the boat's lights fade as they traveled farther and farther away, until they were nothing more than pinpoints of light on the dark waves.

The helicopter veered toward the boat, and Nicky felt a rush of adrenaline. She clenched her jaw, trying to stay calm.

They followed the boat, staying back, but close enough to keep track of it.

It was a little boat. Nicky didn't know what type, but it was definitely one that she could set on fire. A sinking feeling settled into her stomach at the thought.

They followed it for what seemed like forever. The helicopter raced through the dark sky, going quickly. Nicky wished she could see the island. She tried to look, but it was impossible to see, even with the moon.

Nicky's heart was pounding in her ears. It was almost deafening. She still didn't know how they were going to get Natalia back—they could be miles away from the island, and at this point, they were on a different body of water. She had no idea how they were going to get Natalia out of there. Would they try to get her out of the boat? Free her when they got on land?

The boat was getting closer to the shore.

"Hold on!" Danny shouted. The helicopter dipped, getting closer to the boat. Nicky saw the kidnappers, who had Natalia bound and gagged on the boat. Natalia was terrified, her eyes scrunched up, her body shaking.

But she was alive.

Now, they needed to catch that damn boat.

CHAPTER TWENTY FIVE

"Hurry, Danny!" Nicky shouted at the pilot, but the boat was speeding far away from the island now—like it was trying to escape.

"I'm trying!" Danny said, shouting back. "The winds are really strong—"

"—and that boat is fast," Rachel said.

Nicky was clenching her teeth as hard as she could. She was nervous. She felt cold. She was having trouble breathing. It felt like her heart was being squeezed in a vice. She told herself that Natalia was alive. They had to be close to catching them. They were in a helicopter, after all.

They were close enough that the kidnappers must have seen them—they veered the boat around and sped back to the island.

"Stay with them!" Nicky said. She leaned forward. She was gripping the seat in front of her so tightly that her knuckles were white. Natalia was right there. They had to get her.

"I'm trying!" Danny said.

There was urgency in the pilot's voice, and it made Nicky's stomach sink in a new way. She was afraid that they weren't going to be able to catch up to the boat in time. She was afraid that they weren't going to be able to get to the boat at all.

But then, right as she was about to give up hope, she saw something on the boat—something that made her heart drop.

"Oh, no," she said. "Oh, no."

Her heart sank even further.

She watched as the boat veered off into the open sea, far away from the land. A man stood up from the boat—his hands high in the air—but then she realized what he was holding.

A gun.

As they helicopter soared toward the boat, a shot was fired into the air. "Shit!" Danny yelled. The helicopter swayed as he dodged the hit. Down below, the boat turned away again.

The chase was back on.

Nicky looked at Natalia, sitting on the boat. Her hands bound, and her face covered in tears. She was trying to show Nicky that she was still alive and still fighting to be found. Nicky saw it all, and her heart sank even further.

The lights on the boat were fading. It was getting easier and easier to lose sight of it. The helicopter was going too fast to keep up—the boat was flying away, getting farther and farther away from the land.

The kidnappers were getting away.

"We're losing them!" Nicky said. "We're going to lose them."

The helicopter zoomed along, almost hitting the boat several times.

"Damn!" Danny shouted. Another shot was fired from the boat.

"This guy is good," Danny said. "I can't fly this so close to the water—if we get one more hit, I'm going to have to pull away."

"Not yet!" Nicky shouted. "He's not getting away!"

The helicopter sped away from the boat. The kidnapper's shots were missing, but only just barely.

Danny pulled away, then returned, and then pulled away again. A third shot went wild. Then he closed the distance again.

Nicky's heart rate was so high that she felt like she couldn't breathe. She could barely hear the roar of the helicopter. She could barely feel the wind. A lingering fog, along with a dull pain, ached through her head.

She kept her eyes fixed on the boat.

Nicky could feel herself breathing hard—like she had just sprinted a hundred yards. She felt like she was going to throw up. The helicopter was flying effortlessly through the sky. Nicky was not feeling the same ease. She was nervous. She was afraid. And she was angry—so angry that she could barely think.

Then, as Danny swooped down again, the boat geared back around. This time, it was heading straight for the island.

"They're heading back!" Nicky said. She pressed her face to the binoculars. "It was a feint!"

They had to catch up to the boat, fast.

"They're getting away!" Rachel said.

"I know!" Nicky said. "We have to get them."

Nicky could see the determination in Rachel's eyes—she knew that Rachel was on board with this, ready to bring Natalia home.

Danny steered the helicopter after the boat. Natalia was still standing up on the boat, her hands bound, her head covered. She was clutching the edge of the boat, looking back at the island, at Nicky.

Nicky's fists were clenched together so tightly that her fingers were turning white. She was so scared that she felt like she might throw up.

She didn't know if the helicopter would be able to catch the boat. But she knew that the kidnappers were counting on it.

The kidnappers were counting on the fact that they wouldn't be able to catch them. If they couldn't catch them, then they would go back to the island.

And that would be the end.

But Nicky knew that they couldn't let that happen.

"Go, Danny!" she said. "Go!"

But the boat was speeding, fast, toward the island—showing no sign of letting up.

"They're gonna crash the boat!" Nicky screamed.

They were insane. Mindless. They were going to crash the boat right into the shore—with Natalia on it.

Nicky watched through the binoculars as the boat got closer and closer.

"It's not going to stop!" Rachel said.

Nicky watched through the binoculars as the boat raced toward the island. She was screaming.

"Stop! Stop! Stop!"

The boat plowed right into the island, the hull breaking apart with a splash. Instantly, smoke rose from it, but there was no explosion.

"Shit!" Danny said. "The son of a bitch is going to kill her!"

The kidnappers were counting on that.

The kidnappers were counting on the fact that they wouldn't be able to catch them.

That it would be over.

"We need to land," Nicky shouted to Danny. "Land us on shore, as close to the boat as possible."

If the kidnappers and Natalia were still alive, then they would probably try to make a run for it. Maybe they'd leave Natalia behind.

And if Nicky and the others were able to reach Natalia before they did, they could save her.

They could still do this.

As they flew closer to the island, Nicky looked down at the boat—the kidnappers' plan was obvious. The boat was still smoking, but Marissa and James were gone. The kidnappers had fled the scene.

"Shit," Nicky said. "I don't see them."

The kidnappers were gone.

And so was Natalia.

Nicky felt her heart sink—she couldn't stand it. She didn't want it to be over. This wasn't over.

But what choice did they have?

They couldn't let Marissa and James get away. And they couldn't leave Natalia behind. They had to go back to the island.

And so, Nicky slumped back in the seat and looked out the window, watching the island get closer and closer. They had to land. They had to go back to the island and finish this.

They had to save Natalia.

They couldn't let the kidnappers win.

Nicky felt like she was going to throw up. She felt sick. She stared out the window and watched the island come closer.

They had to do this.

CHAPTER TWENTY SIX

The rotors of the helicopter slowed to a stop, their familiar high-pitched whine changing pitch as they slowed. The engine revved. The pilot lowered the craft until the skids kissed the shore of the island and then shut off the engine.

The moment the helicopter stopped, Nicky unstrapped herself and hurried off the helicopter. Ken was right behind her, and they both scrambled onto the sand of the beach, heading in the direction that the boat had crashed in.

Nicky's heart was beating so fast that she felt like she was going to throw up. She was terrified that Natalia was already dead. Marissa and James had to have escaped. The kidnappers had to be on the run.

The smoke was rising even higher—the boat's fire had caught, no doubt because of the gasoline. Nicky and Ken rushed up to the wreckage, but there was no sign of any people anywhere near it.

"Where are they?" Nicky said. "Where are they?"

"Maybe they're hiding," Ken said.

Nicky and Ken searched the boat, which was still smoking. The hull had been completely smashed by the crash—the boat wasn't going anywhere, and the kidnappers were gone.

They were gone.

Nicky looked at the sand. It was hard to see in the darkness, and the clouds blotted out the moon, but she could see footprints.

"That way," Nicky said, pointing toward the forest. "They went into the woods!"

Nicky ran as fast as she could. She was out of breath and her heart was beating hard, but she kept running. Her fear for Natalia was propelling her forward. They had to catch the kidnappers. She couldn't let them get away.

As Nicky and Ken entered the forest, the cloudy night sky peered through the clouds, shining down on the trees and the ground. The kidnappers were nowhere to be seen. The footprints led in a single, straight line, and Nicky and the others followed behind, trying to keep pace but struggling to do so. Marissa and James were moving fast. They must have untied Natalia and were dragging her with them. There was no blood, so Nicky could only hold onto hope that Natalia was still alive.

They charged through the forest, following the trail of footprints. James and Marissa were moving with great ease through the trees, and Nicky and Ken had to struggle to keep up. Nicky felt like she was going to throw up. She didn't want to lose this. She didn't want to lose Natalia.

She couldn't let Marissa and James get away with this.

The footprints led up a steep hill through the trees. Nicky didn't stop to catch her breath. She kept running. She kept pushing forward. She had to catch the kidnappers. She had to save Natalia. She didn't care how far they ran—she just knew that she had to catch up to them.

The footprints kept leading up the hill. Nicky and Ken were struggling to keep up—the kidnappers were moving too fast. But Nicky and Ken didn't care. They kept running. They had to reach Natalia before Marissa and James killed her. They had to stop this.

She kept following the footsteps through the woods. The kidnappers didn't seem to be slowing down, but Nicky and the others were struggling to keep pace with them.

The trail of footprints led Nicky and the others around a few trees and down a steep hill. Suddenly, the footsteps stopped. Nicky and Ken hurried forward, both out of breath, and stopped by the footprints. The kidnappers were gone. The footsteps stopped in the middle of nowhere, as if the kidnappers had simply disappeared.

Natalia was gone.

"They must have stopped here," Ken said. "They must have ditched her and continued on."

"No," Nicky said. "I don't think so. If they wanted to get farther away from us, they would have gone in the other direction. The way they were going before was taking them to the end of the island."

"You're right," Ken said.

Nicky tried to catch her breath. She had been running through the forest so fast that it was taking her a moment to regulate her breathing.

She felt like she was going to be sick. She didn't know what to do. She had to find Natalia.

"I'll go check down the hill," Ken said. "You go ahead. Check above us."

Nicky nodded. She felt sick. She didn't want to leave Natalia behind, but she didn't have a choice. She had to go forward. She had to find the kidnappers.

Ken headed back down the hill. Nicky climbed to the top of the hill and peered through the trees, looking for any sign of Marissa and James. She shined her flashlight in every direction, but she didn't see anything. They must have thrown Natalia down the hill and continued forward.

Nicky was tired. She wanted to go home. She wanted to go to bed and rest. She didn't want to be awake and have to deal with the reality that she might not save Natalia Cavazos.

She might lose the vice president's daughter.

But she didn't have a choice. She had to keep going. She had to stay awake.

She kept looking through the trees. This wasn't working. They needed to keep pushing. They needed to track them down, but it was so damn dark. With the clouds blocking the sky, not even the moon was there to guide Nicky.

Maybe she was going about this wrong.

She had to start thinking instead of running around aimlessly.

Marissa and James had taken Natalia, and they needed to get away from Nicky and Ken. They needed to get out of the forest, and they needed to get away from the island. They needed to hide.

If Nicky was going to catch them, she would need to understand their mindset.

They went somewhere. They went somewhere nearby, and Nicky and Ken had to find that place.

Nicky's eyes were weary. She was exhausted, but she had to keep going. She had to push on. She had to get her mind off of being tired.

The kidnappers had to be hiding in a place nearby. They had to be.

Nicky kept climbing the hill, desperately hoping to find something. She stopped when she realized that she heard something.

A sound.

A voice.

Nicky froze.

She listened.

It was a voice.

Someone was hurt.

Someone was struggling.

Someone was crying.

Nicky listened.

The crying was coming from her right. She followed the sound of the crying all the way to her left and then back to her right.

She kept moving, only listening.

The crying was getting louder.

The person was getting closer. Nicky tried to figure out where the sound was coming from. It was almost directly to her right.

She dashed through the trees, and that was when she saw it.

It was James. And he was holding a knife to Natalia's throat.

CHAPTER TWENTY SEVEN

The stillness of the forest wrapped around Nicky like a thick, dark blanket. The night was so quiet that she could hear her own heart beating. She stopped, the sweat pools stinging her eyes, and tried to peer through the darkness. Nothing moved in the shadows. Nothing. But she was not alone.

"Drop the gun!" James shouted. "Drop it or Natalia dies!"

There was a knife to Natalia's throat. It was a folding knife, but James held it firmly against Natalia's throat. If Nicky made a move, he would kill her.

She could feel her heart beating fast. It was beating faster than ever before.

Nicky dropped her gun.

She had to think of something.

She had to think fast.

She didn't know what to do.

"Don't come any closer," James said. His voice was raspy. He was clearly panicked. "I will kill her."

"Don't do this," Nicky said. "There's no reason to hurt her."

"I don't care about her," James said. "I just care about me. I just care about my sister."

Marissa wasn't anywhere in sight. Then, in the distance, the sound of a gun resounded through the air. Natalia flinched. Nicky didn't know what to think, but she could assume one of two things.

One: Ken had found and shot Marissa.

Two: Marissa had the gun, and she shot at Ken.

Worry took hold of Nicky. If something happened to Ken while they were split up, she could never forgive herself.

But right now, she had to stay in the moment. Natalia Cavazos was alive, right in front of her. But not for long if she didn't talk James off this ledge.

She had no idea how to get in his head, though. Nothing was known about James. He looked young and scared, a twenty-year-old boy who bore so much resemblance to Natalia that it was jarring.

He really was her brother.

Nicky doubted a kid like him had ever been in trouble with the law before, and now he was about to murder his own half-sister. Maybe Nicky could use that.

"James," Nicky said slowly. "It's okay. You don't have to do this. You're not a killer. You've never killed before..."

She had to get him to think clearly. He was panicking. He was going to make a mistake.

Nicky needed him to listen to her.

She needed him to stop.

But his eyes were wild.

"Shut up!" James said. "You don't know anything about my past."

"I know you're not a killer," Nicky said. "I know you don't want to do this. You're scared. But we can get through this together. We can. Just put the knife down. You can come with me. Nobody has to die."

James shook his head. "No. You don't get it. I can't go back. I can't go back to the life I had. I need this."

"You don't need to kill Natalia," Nicky said. "You don't need to kill anyone. Come with me. Please, James."

"No!" His voice came out harsh. "Do you have any idea how I feel? How my sister feels? We spent our whole lives believing we didn't have a father and now—" He took a breath. "Our mother told us our father was dead, but he's not. He's Steven fucking Cavazos."

Underneath James, Natalia's eyes widened. Evidently, she hadn't yet learned that she had two half-siblings—and that they'd kidnapped her.

"W…what?" Natalia managed, tears streaming down her pale cheeks.

"That's right, sister," James sneered. "Your precious daddy is our daddy too. He had an affair with our mother. He tried to keep us a secret, but no—my mother told us the truth. And now I know. Now I see it. My father was living this perfect fairy tale life in the public eye with this stupid bitch as his daughter, while pretending that my beautiful sister and I don't even exist! When he's the vice president of the United States!"

Nicky took a breath. James's anger was peaking. In truth, she understood him.

She thought of her own father.

How much of a deadbeat he was. How much of a disappointment he was.

"I get you, James," Nicky said, holding up her hands. "My father—he let me down too. He was never there for my sister and me."

"No, he wasn't," James agreed. "He—"

The words didn't come out of his mouth. He started to lose his grasp on Natalia.

"He's a liar," James said instead. "Like I said, he lied to us. I hate him. I hate him so much."

"I know you do," Nicky said. "But you don't have to kill Natalia to get him back."

James's face turned white. "I can't let him get away with this," he said. "I can't. I know you don't understand. I know you don't feel it. But I have so much rage inside of me."

"I understand," Nicky said. "I do. But we can't let our anger control us. That's what our fathers have done. We have to make a stand. We have to take our lives back."

"Well, I can't take my life back," James said. "I can't return to the life I had. It's over. This is it."

"You don't have to live your life alone," Nicky said. "You don't want to hurt Natalia. You don't want to kill your sister. You don't want to lose someone you love."

Natalia's eyes were pleading. There were tears streaming down her cheeks. Her eyes were wide. She was clearly pleading for Nicky to save her. She was clearly begging for Nicky to make it stop.

"I do," James said. "I do want to hurt her. I want to see her bleed. I want to see her cry. I want to see her die. And I want to see my father die. I want to ruin all of their lives—the people who have hurt me, the people who have hurt my mother, and the people who have hurt my sister."

Nicky tried to keep her voice soft and quiet. She didn't want to make James angrier. She didn't want to make him lose his cool.

She had to get him to put the knife down.

She had to get him to let Natalia go.

"James," Nicky said, "Natalia—she must feel so betrayed too."

Nicky locked eyes with Natalia, who shot her a confused look. Nicky gave her a subtle nod, urging her to play along. It was their only shot.

"Her father lied to her too," Nicky told James. "Natalia is only now finding out that her perfect, politician father had another family he never told her about. Don't you think Natalia would have wanted to know that? Don't you think she would have wanted to know her siblings? You look just like her..."

That seemed to strike a chord in James. His expression morphed into something more confused.

"Y…yes," Natalia managed, the knife still at her throat. "I am so betrayed. I wish I had known you..."

"Bullshit," James uttered. "You don't care. You got to live in the public eye as his perfect princess. Marissa and I had nothing!"

"I was so lonely," Natalia said through her tears. "So lonely, James. My father was so overbearing. He tried to control my every move. It wasn't as perfect as the media made it seem, I promise..."

"You don't...you don't know how good you had it," James said. "You don't know how lucky you are. I had to hear the rumors. I had to hear the speculation. Everyone was always talking about you and your dad. About how perfect you were. And I had to hear it every day. I had to hear it every day and he never even gave me a chance."

Nicky kept her eyes locked on James. He was a ticking time bomb.

She didn't know where this was going to go next, but she knew that if she didn't get him to put down his knife, James was going to get even angrier—and he was going to kill his sister.

"James," Nicky said, "Natalia—she must have been so afraid. I mean, she didn't know anything. She didn't know what you and your mother were going through. She didn't know about your father. She didn't know about her brother and sister."

"You don't have to do this," Natalia said, her voice shaking. "You're right. I got to live in the public eye as his daughter. But I do care about you. I do care about my family. And I care about the pain you're feeling. I feel it too."

"No, you don't," James told her. "You've had everything handed to you. You and your father have gotten away with murder."

"I'm not saying I don't deserve some of the blame for that," Natalia said. "But you and your sister, you deserve so much better than what you had. You are so much more than your circumstances. You are so much more than the way you've been treated. You can fight back. You can fight back against the people who have hurt you. You can hurt them back—but in a way that's not destructive. By destroying their lives, you're only hurting yourself. You're only disrespecting yourself."

As Natalia was talking, Nicky was impressed at her ability to keep herself together. Slowly, Nicky inched closer to them. The moment

James lowered the knife, she could get in and disarm him, and this would all be over.

Another gunshot was heard in the distance.

Nicky tensed up. She was ready to spring into action. She was ready to disarm him.

But he didn't drop the knife. Instead, he clutched it tighter and said, "I'm going to get my revenge. I'm going to get my revenge on everyone who has wronged me. I'm going to kill them all."

"James," Nicky said, "put the knife down. You don't want to hurt your sister. Please, James. Please. I know it hurts. I know you're angry. But—"

Nicky moved in closer. She inched toward James and Natalia. She moved toward James. At the same time, Nicky could hear helicopters flying in, and she could see spotlights illuminating in the distance.

And from the look on James's face, he could hear it too.

"They're coming," James said, sounding defeated. "They're here. The police...they're here to take me away. Damn it. Damn it, I don't want to go to jail—"

He started to shake his head. Nicky could tell he was trying to think of a way out. His grip on the knife started to loosen.

"Let's go," Nicky said, trying to sound as convincing as possible. "We should go. We should get out of here. We can leave. It's not too late. We can leave together."

"I—"

"Let's get out of here," Nicky said again. "You don't want to go to jail. Neither of us do. Let's get out of here. Let's go."

James's face flickered with a moment of indecision. Perhaps he was reconsidering his actions. Perhaps he was trying to figure out what he had gotten himself into.

It was enough for Nicky. She knew she had to strike.

CHAPTER TWENTY EIGHT

Darkness surrounded Ken as he tore through the forest with tunnel vision. He'd heard her up ahead—the footsteps of the other girl, trying to escape. He had his gun out, channeling his years of training in the FBI to tear through the damp jungle.

She wouldn't get away with this. This girl—Marissa—was guilty of kidnapping the vice president's daughter as much as her brother, and Ken wouldn't stand for it.

He couldn't.

Ken's breath fogged up in the humid air. The rain was starting, and an eerie blue hue was starting to sweep through the sky. He kept running, hopping over a branch as he dodged around foliage. He had a trail on the girl—he could still hear her, up ahead, but he didn't have eyes on her. Damn it.

He heard a gunshot, and Ken got a chill. He immediately started looking around to his left, desperately trying to find a break in the foliage between the trees.

What was he doing? He couldn't see her, but he was sure that girl couldn't still be up ahead. He'd heard what sounded like a gunshot up ahead and he couldn't even see any signs of the girl since then—couldn't see any movement. Maybe she'd left? Maybe she'd run off somewhere else? But if that was the case...where had the gunshot come from?

Ken trudged through the jungle, digging his feet into the mud as he kicked away tree branches, springing to his feet as another gunshot was heard in the distance. It wasn't coming from the direction Nicky was in, which meant it couldn't be from her.

Maybe he was wrong. Maybe Marissa had gone that way.

Ken took a breath and followed the direction of the gunshot, navigating the dark woods, his heart pounding heavily in his chest.

There was a break in the foliage. Ken squinted and forced himself forward, holding his gun out, ready to shoot. Crazies were known for shooting anyone, but especially anyone trying to chase them down.

Ken took a breath and focused. He realized that there were two sets of footsteps on the ground.

He couldn't tell if it was two people or just one person walking back and forth. He needed to get closer.

Ken dug his feet into the mud and forced himself forward through the break in the foliage.

And there, in the clearing, he saw her: the girl, Marissa. Natalia's half-sister. They looked so much alike that it shocked Ken. But unlike Natalia, Marissa had an emptiness on her face. She stood there in the moonlight, fists balled at her sides.

But Ken didn't see the gun. Maybe she dropped it?

He stepped into the clearing, holding his gun out. Marissa looked at him, unafraid.

"Marissa, this ends here," Ken said. "I'm with the FBI. You can't escape this."

Marissa shook her head.

"Damn it, listen to me!" Ken shouted. "You kidnapped the daughter of the vice president! You have no choice but to face the consequences!"

"I am the vice president's daughter," Marissa countered.

Ken advanced on Marissa cautiously. "You can come peacefully if you want or you can come the hard way," Ken said. "Your choice."

Marissa laughed, and Ken couldn't help but think that this girl was completely out of her mind. Her eyes were filled with a deranged happiness, like this was all a game to her.

"Oh, you pathetic FBI agent," she said. "Don't you know you're a pawn to them? The government—people like my father—would throw you away the moment you didn't serve them anymore. Why do you serve them, Agent?"

"I serve justice," Ken said. "Justice, Marissa. Justice."

A crazy smile spread across Marissa's face and Ken lowered his gun. This girl didn't seem like she was armed. He could tackle her right now, grab her and hold her down until the choppers arrived to pick them both up.

"Justice is a false concept," Marissa said. "It doesn't exist. It's a concept created by people who want to take control of their lives, who want to tell others what they can and cannot do and what they should and shouldn't believe in. They will enslave you with words like justice, words like revenge. You've been so brainwashed that you're willing to shoot someone because someone said you should shoot them."

"Believing in justice doesn't mean I have to go around hurting people!" Ken said angrily. "I don't want to shoot you, Marissa. I just want you to pay for what you did to Natalia Cavazos."

"Like a good little pawn," Marissa said.

"Just come peacefully and I'll make sure you get a better deal than James," Ken said.

"If I'm guilty, then so are you, Agent. Because you're taking someone's side—the side of their family and their friends...the side of all those who believe in goodness and justice, who believe that everyone should live some sort of happy, rewarding life where we experience and see life as it should be for everyone...but it's not like that for everyone, is it? What about my brother and I?"

"You were spoiled brats," Ken said. "I don't pity you. Now stop messing around." He reached into his back pocket, pulling out cuffs. "I'm going to arrest you, Marissa."

Another smile curled at her lips. "Is that so?"

Then, her eyes flickered behind Ken.

Like she was looking at someone.

Ken's instincts ignited. He spun around—only to hear the loud bang of a gun.

Something molten hot pierced through his left side. Ken had been shot before, and the feeling ignited every nerve in his body, but he was in shock. Because Marissa, standing before him, had no weapon.

The shot had come from behind.

Ken turned around to see a man he'd never seen before standing there. A guy with a mustache, tattoos, and a military vest.

What the...?

Ken turned back to Marissa. She had a manic smile on her face. "You heard me, Agent," she said. "Justice doesn't exist. And you trust all these men who live off the backs of systems created by groups of men...which don't exist either."

Ken's mind whirred. There was so much noise. So much weakness in his body. He could feel the blood gushing out, hot and warm, but the pain barely registered over the shock.

His head went light. He had no choice but to collapse onto the ground.

They're not alone. The thought moved through his mind, and in that moment, all he could think about was Nicky.

She wouldn't be prepared for this either.

Ken lay back on the grass. Above him, the stars. Then, Marissa's face and the face of the other man—the unknown man.

"Do we finish him off?" Marissa asked.

"He won't last," said the man. "Leave him."

Was this really the end? Ken was still breathing—still thinking—but everything felt so dull. As their footsteps left him there in the clearing, Ken's thoughts began to race. He couldn't just give up. He hadn't dedicated his life to the FBI to be shot by someone in the woods, on some island, and bleed out like a fool.

With the only strength he had, Ken dragged himself away from the clearing and rested against the base of a tree. He held his hand over his wound. It was on the left side. If they'd hit his heart, he'd already be dead. No, it was a shoulder wound. Close. And he was losing blood.

But he had to hope that he'd make it.

But when he went to move his arm, to call for backup, he found that he was paralyzed.

His arm was there, by his side, but it wasn't moving.

It took everything in Ken's willpower not to cry out. He had to stay awake, and he had to keep thinking of ways out of this situation.

He brought his phone to the front and tried to turn it on, but its screen was shattered.

Damn it.

Ken looked around again. No one was in sight.

If no one came back to get him, he could easily bleed out here without anyone knowing.

Nothing was working. He couldn't move.

He tried to drag the arm over, to activate his earpiece, but nothing was working. He heard a small laugh.

"I'm going to die," he thought weakly.

He looked past the base of the tree and stared at the moon. Another gunshot in the distance. The time passed slowly, minutes ticking by as Ken's vision began to blur as his consciousness left him and darkness took over.

Visions of his life sped before his eyes. Back in high school, when his girlfriend had been murdered. Ken had never loved again. The pain was too much. He became an FBI agent to save more girls like her, but he hadn't planned on dying. Not yet.

He thought of Nicky. Of her brown eyes and long, silky hair. Of her tenacity. He had to admit that he'd grown fond of her since they became partners. She was beautiful. In fact, she was the only person who he'd truly felt something for since he was a teenager.

She was a true partner. That he'd been thinking of a life beyond the FBI with her wasn't a farce or a joke.

Nicky...

The pain in his shoulder was too much. He couldn't make out the stars. Ken closed his eyes as the darkness filled his body and mind.

CHAPTER TWENTY NINE

Springing forward, Nicky jumped up toward James and Natalia, putting her hands up, and effectively knocked the knife out of James's hand.

Natalia fell to the floor with a thud, and James stumbled back.

As she was falling, Nicky's eyes met with James's. A look of hatred crossed his expression, and as he took a swing at her, Nicky instinctively flinched.

She caught herself. She was ready to fight him off.

She grabbed onto James's shoulders, trying to hold him back and trying to take him down.

But James was strong. He was surprisingly strong. He was able to hold his own against Nicky.

She had been able to take him by surprise, but she couldn't hold him down.

Natalia let out a scream. Nicky tried to hold onto James, but he was able to shake her off.

She flew back, landing hard on the ground. She winced as she hit the earth.

At that moment, the vibrations through her body reverberated straight to her skull, reawakening the injury from earlier. The back of her head throbbed, and Nicky saw stars.

No. I can't give up.

She rocked to her feet as James ran off into the woods. Nicky's head pounded, but she dashed after him.

"James. James, stop running!"

She had to catch him. If she lost him now, she wasn't sure that they'd find him again.

"James, stop!"

She had the attention of the cops, but she wasn't sure how long it would last.

"James!"

She kept running, but he was fading into the woods.

Fading away.

Nicky picked up her pace. Adrenaline surged through her. This was it. She had to catch him.

If she didn't, it would all be for nothing. She would have failed.

She was still in pain. Her head was still hurting. She was still in danger of losing him.

But she had to keep going.

She had to make it work.

Picking up her speed, she ran faster. She ignored her aching head. She ignored the throbbing in her leg. She ignored the exhaustion in her body.

She had to catch him.

With branches snagging at her shirt, she continued to chase after James.

She felt like she was chasing after an animal.

She had to catch him. She couldn't give up now. She had to catch him.

The moment that she was close enough, Nicky dove forward, tackling James from behind and bringing him straight to the ground.

With the last bit of her strength, Nicky slapped cuffs on his wrists.

"It's over, James," she said, huffing. "It's over."

***

Nicky hauled James down to the beach, where the police helicopters and the Coast Guard were waiting, their lights illuminating the dark night. Natalia was behind Nicky, and the whole time they'd walked, she'd been telling Nicky how grateful—and shocked—she was. All the while, James had stayed resentfully quiet, allowing himself to be hauled down to the beach.

As soon as Nicky, Natalia, and James reached the shore, several secret service agents poured out of their helicopter. They spotted Natalia. It was Agent Turner and Agent Thomas.

Nicky was still holding onto James, and Natalia slowly started to run toward the two agents.

As soon as they saw her, they ran at her too.

"Ms. Cavazos!" they called out.

"Ms. Cavazos, are you all right?"

"Yes," Natalia said, barely able to contain her excitement. "Agent Turner, Agent Thomas, I'm fine. I'm so glad to see you. I'm so relieved that you're here."

"But we lost you," Agent Turner said, hanging his head low in shame. "We failed you."

The two agents crowded around Natalia, checking her over and making sure she was in one piece. The relief on Agent Turner's face was plain to see.

Nicky let out a sigh as she pulled James away, leaving Natalia and the secret service agents to work things out.

Several police officers swarmed the area, and when they saw Nicky, they jogged over to her. Nicky literally shoved James at them, and they caught him, looking at her like deer caught in the headlights.

"This is James Gibbons," Nicky said.

"Thank you," the officer stammered.

Nicky put her hands on her waist and looked around the beach. It was crowded with officials.

But she didn't see Ken and Marissa anywhere.

"Was the other one brought in?" she asked the officer.

"Other one?" the officer asked.

"There were two," Nicky said, her heart sinking. "He had an accomplice. A sister. My partner went after her..."

"Ma'am, we haven't seen them..."

Nicky's stomach dropped. She thought of the gunshots that they'd heard in the woods.

If Ken didn't have Marissa back by now, then that could mean...

That could mean she shot him and escaped.

"I need every man you have scouring the woods, now," Nicky said. "We might have a federal agent in danger. And a fugitive is still on the lose."

The officer nodded. "Ma'am, we're on it."

With that, Nicky ran back into the woods.

Exhausted, Nicky found herself in a part of the woods that she didn't recognize. She had been running around for what felt like hours. She hadn't seen or heard anyone—human or otherwise—in quite a while.

She wasn't sure how much time she had left. She wasn't sure what was going to happen. She didn't know if it was over or if she should keep looking.

The lack of answers and the prospect of failure was making her lose hope. She didn't know what to do. The nightmare was still creeping up on her.

She had no idea what to do. But she had to find Ken. She had to make sure he was okay.

If something happened to him...

No. Nicky couldn't bear to think it. She felt like she was just getting to know Ken Walker, and to lose him…she couldn't let it happen.

He was in these woods somewhere. And so was Marissa.

Nicky had to find them. She had to help him.

And if I fail...

She couldn't fail. She refused to fail. Not when she was so close to success.

Nicky's whole body ached as she pushed through the woods. She was ready to drop, but she refused to give up hope.

Then, suddenly, a gunshot whirred past her, shocking Nicky so much that she fell backwards and landed on the cool grass. Ducking away, Nicky rolled into the bushes and pulled out her weapon, her mind suddenly on high alert. She crouched in the bush, holding her gun up, her heart thundering in her ears.

Who had shot at her?

"Marissa," Nicky said, her voice trembling. "I know you're out there. Come out."

There was more chaos in the distance—the sound of an officer yelling. Then, a female-sounding shout. As though an officer had found Marissa and got her...

But if that was the case, and Marissa was caught…

Then who just shot her?

Nicky swallowed, her mouth dry at the fear of the unknown.

She braced her weapon, ready to shoot anything that would emerge from the trees.

The confusion made her feel sick. But the thought that she may have just lost again—and got an innocent person, Ken, hurt—made her want to cry. She wanted to cry in frustration. Because how could she have let this happen?

"I will shoot if you don't come out," Nicky said, her voice wavering.

She had no idea what would happen if she fired, but she honestly didn't care anymore at this point. She just wanted her partner back and to know they had won.

Slowly, a lone figure appeared near the edge of the woods. A male figure. Tall, slender...

Nicky squinted. She had no idea who this was. He was wearing a military vest, had tattoos up his thin arms, and a mustache lined his lip. He had ratty brown hair and dark, sinister eyes. A hunting rifle was slung over his shoulder.

"Oh, to hell with it all," the man said. "Come out and play with me. I'm dying for a rush."

"Who the hell are you?" Nicky called out, still hidden in the bush. "What the hell are you doing here?"

"You really thought those two idiots orchestrated this alone?" the man taunted. "The girl—Natalia Cavazos—she was supposed to come to me. I'd fetch a pretty penny for returning her body to her father..." He paused. Nicky's heart raced. "But it all fell apart."

She couldn't believe it. They had an accomplice. This person, this man—he must have been waiting here for James and Marissa to deliver Natalia. By the sounds of it, he hadn't planned to let her live and would ransom her body back to her father so that he could bury her.

The thought made her sick.

But she had to move forward. Nicky couldn't spend her time feeling sick and angry, not when there was a dangerous killer loose in the woods.

It wasn't over yet. And Nicky was determined to win.

She had to find Ken.

"So what are you doing here, shitbag?" Nicky demanded. "It's over. Natalia's safe. James and Marissa are done. Why are you here?"

She watched, heart pounding, as the person moved out of the darkness into a nearby clearing. He still looked shady and imposing in the moonlight.

Then, he laughed. "I haven't had this much fun since I was in the war."

All of a sudden, he disappeared into the bushes.

Nicky's heart stalled.

She couldn't see him.

And he was a trained soldier. To make it worse, she had no idea where he would appear.

She suspected that he was just toying with her, giving her a false sense of security.

"Where are you?!" she demanded, forcing herself to stay calm as she scanned the bushes around her. "Just tell me why you're here!"

The man circled Nicky. He was like a lion hunting a deer, cutting off her escape and closing in for the kill.

Nicky swallowed back her fear. She watched the man carefully, and then when she saw him back-peddling out of the corner of her eye, she bolted. She didn't want to be trapped in the clearing with someone like that lurking around her.

She ran across a nearby clearing, ducking under branches as she went. But she didn't hear any following footsteps behind her—and it made her too afraid to stop running.

She had no idea where he was going to attack from next—or even if he really intended to do her harm. But something about him made her sick in the stomach.

If Ken wasn't here, Nicky could only assume that this guy had gotten the upper hand on him.

A bullet fired through the forest again, and Nicky jumped out of the way. She whirled around and shot, but she only had a handgun.

She would have to outsmart him.

Nicky looked up at the trees. She could climb up, get a good vantage point, and then strike.

The man moved toward her, unloading a bullet like he was shooting a machine gun.

Nicky dove in the other direction, right into a tree, and swung herself up onto it. She climbed as quickly as she could, not even daring to look back as she kept climbing. She had to get as far away from him as possible.

From his position on the ground, the man laughed maniacally. Nicky didn't know what he had been upset about, but he clearly was enjoying this.

He just wanted to scare her. He liked seeing her suffer.

She couldn't play his game.

Nicky took a deep, shaky breath as she positioned herself in the tree. Her heart thundered so loud, it overpowered her hearing, but she had to stay calm.

She had to focus.

Closing her eyes, she concentrated on his breathing and footsteps. He was moving toward her. Nicky knew it. And when he moved into another clearing, she tackled him from the tree.

Dust flew everywhere as Nicky crashed down on top of the man in a painful position. She had never been in a battle like this before, and she immediately wished she was wearing a vest and a helmet because falling on the ground hurt even more than she had anticipated.

The man squirmed under her, trying to get up. Nicky tried to keep him pinned down, but his feet pushed against hers as he tried to get away from her grip.

There was no room for hesitation.

As soon as Nicky balanced on her feet, she fired a shot right at the man.

He looked down, stunned, like he hadn't expected it. Nicky breathed heavily, sweat pooling at her brow and dripping down her forehead. Blood blossomed on the man's vest, right in the middle of his chest, and he looked up at Nicky with a wide, crazed smile.

"Finally..." He trailed off before he collapsed to the ground, falling face-first into the grass.

Nicky's chest heaved. He was dead. It was over. Adrenaline coursed through her, but a moment of reality reminded her that this wasn't over. Not at all.

She still had to find Ken.

Without thinking, Nicky dove off.

CHAPTER THIRTY

Nicky kept running through the woods, through the darkness, hoping—praying—that Ken was alive. She didn't have time to think about what she'd done, that she'd just killed a man in the woods. There was no time.

Please be okay, Ken. Please be alive.

Her legs hurt as she ran and ran. "Walker!" she shouted out. Her voice came out raw and painful.

Then, as she skidded into a clearing, she heard it:

A ragged, masculine grunt.

"Ken!" Nicky called out.

She waited, listening to the sounds of the forest.

Then, like a beacon of light, she heard his voice:

"Lyons, o…over..."

"Ken, where are you!?" Nicky called out. She kept running in the direction of the sound.

"O…over..." His voice was louder now, but still weak.

He sounded hurt.

Nicky could hear the other officers running through the forest. She could see their flashlights flicker between the trees. One of the helicopters soared over head, looking for Marissa, and Nicky prayed that they'd find her.

She had to find Ken first.

"Ken!" she called out.

This time, he didn't reply. Nicky frantically spun around, surrounded by trees. She kept running in the direction that she swore she heard him, until finally, she reached a clearing.

And there, leaning against a tree, was Ken.

A large patch of blood seeped out of his shoulder.

He'd been shot.

"Ken!" Nicky yelled, running toward him.

With a hand on her chest, she hunched over next to him. "Oh my God, Ken. Oh my God."

The sight of him wounded and hurt—it almost brought tears to Nicky's eyes. She wanted to hold him, to tell him that she was there, and that everything would be okay. Instead, she pulled out her phone to call for backup.

"Nicky," he said, looking up at her and wincing. "You shouldn't...there's another..."

He struggled to say anything more, but he just grimaced in pain.

"I'm here," Nicky said. "It's okay. I'm here."

She didn't know why she said that. She didn't know if it was going to be okay or not.

But it was the only thing she could think to say.

And it was true. She was there. She wasn't going anywhere.

"I can't feel my legs," Ken said. His voice was just above a whisper.

Tears welled up in Nicky's eyes. Her throat felt tight. "You're going to be okay, Ken."

"No," Ken said, shaking his head. "Lyons, you need to leave now."

"No, Ken," she said, smiling. "We caught him. We caught James. We saved Natalia..."

Pale, Ken met her eyes. Nicky could see the light in them fading, and the moment became too real again. She got up and screamed into the forest, "Help! I need help over here!"

There were officers everywhere. Someone had to hear her. They had to come help.

"Nicky," Ken said, his voice barely a whisper.

Nicky got on her knees in front of him again. "Hey, don't worry," she said. She pressed her hands on his wound again, holding it down to stop the blood. "You're gonna be okay, Walker. You're gonna make it."

He laughed a little, then coughed up blood. "You know, I told you before," he said, and their eyes met. "I told you how I had a girlfriend once. She died..."

"I know, Ken. I didn't forget."

"I never cared about anyone ever again," he confessed. "I'm thirty-five, and I never had another girlfriend."

Nicky's heart pounded in her throat. She didn't know where he was going with this, but she wanted to cry.

She didn't want to lose him.

"I never felt anything for anyone ever again," he said, his eyes fluttering shut.

"Walker! Stay with me!" Nicky yelled.

"I never felt it," he mumbled, "until...you..."

Ken's eyes shut.

"Help!" Nicky screamed into the forest, panicking. "Help! Somebody!"

At that moment, two officers ran up with their flashlights.

"Holy shit!" one of them yelled.

"We need a medic, now!" Nicky shouted.

"I'm a paramedic," one of the men said, crouching next to Ken. He took out a syringe and injected it into Ken's arm. "Whoa, he's in bad shape."

"He's bleeding out," Nicky said, trying to stay calm. In her peripheral vision, she could see a helicopter land in the clearing. Paramedics rushed out of it. "He was shot."

"I see that," the paramedic replied. "We're going to move him onto the stretcher. Let's go."

Ken didn't respond as the officers and paramedics worked to move him onto the stretcher.

Nicky stood up and watched as they loaded him into the helicopter.

"He's going to be okay, right?" she asked, pushing the paramedic out of the way.

"I can't tell you that," he said. He was young. He was new. He didn't know.

"Please," Nicky said, tears welling up in her eyes. "Please tell me he's going to be okay!"

"I'm doing the best I can," the paramedic said. "I can see the damage. He's lost a lot of blood, but we'll have him at the hospital in no time."

"Thank you," Nicky said. She watched as the paramedic and officers loaded into the helicopter. She wanted to get in with them. She wanted to go to the hospital with Ken. She wanted to be there when they brought him back.

She wanted a lot of things that she'd never thought she'd want.

But she couldn't deny it anymore.

Somewhere, in all this craziness since the task force was started, Nicky fell for Ken Walker.

Now, she had no idea if he would live or die.

CHAPTER THIRTY ONE

The hospital hallway was dark and still, the lights out at this late hour. A single nurse hurried by, her shoes squeaking on the linoleum floor. Nicky sat in the waiting room, cradling her head between her hands, waiting for news—any news at all.

Even if it was bad.

She jumped at every sound, from the squeak of the nurse's shoes to the elevator doors opening. The waiting room furniture was old and stained. It looked like the chairs had taken on a collective weight—the weight of parents who had sat there while their babies were born, of children who had played and laughed in their short lives, of patients who had spent long hours in that space hoping for good news but knowing that they would find the opposite before long. A calendar on the wall showed a picture of a kitten beneath a rainbow.

It was a nice hospital, she had to admit. But she prayed to God this wouldn't be where Ken Walker let out his last breath.

Nicky had a lot of time to herself in that waiting room.

This entire case had made her think of her father. It was all strange timing; she'd talked to him just the other day, and in twenty-four hours, she'd been sent on a whirlwind of a case that had put her emotions into a blender.

In a way, it made Nicky realize how much pain she'd bottled up about her father for so long.

He was a deadbeat dad. A drunk. He blamed her for her sister's disappearance.

Nicky had been so disappointing in him for so long.

She couldn't meet his standards because he didn't have any—he had let his vices control him. He hadn't even tried to save his family. He had let their good name be destroyed.

In her head, Nicky hadn't forgiven him for any of that.

And yet, in her heart...

In her heart, she did forgive him. In many ways, she hated him, but he was still her father. She had no choice but to love him too.

She'd thought she was strong.

She'd thought she was overcoming the pain of her life, the pain of her childhood, and the pain of being left by her father.

She'd thought she was coming to terms with it.

She'd thought she had dealt with it.

Deep down, she knew that wasn't true.

She was still afraid.

Now, she was afraid that she'd lose Ken too. Nicky didn't have many people in her life. It was hard letting them in. But the way she felt about Ken was different than any partner she'd had before.

Please let him be okay.

"Agent Lyons?"

Nicky lifted her head, hoping to see a doctor or a nurse or someone who could bring her good news.

But to her great shock, it was Vice President Steven Cavazos and Natalia. Behind them were two secret service agents.

Nicky stood up immediately. "Sir..."

Before Nicky could process it, Natalia threw herself at her and hugged her. Nicky was shocked for a moment, but then hugged her back.

"You saved me," Natalia said. "Thank you!"

"Of course," Nicky mumbled.

Natalia broke away with tears in her brown eyes. "I thought those maniacs were going to kill me. I tried to fight them, I really did, but they were too strong for me. But you were able to take them. You're my hero, Agent Lyons."

"I did what I had to do," Nicky said, but she was blushing profusely.

Nicky could remember what it was like to be so young and optimistic, the whole world ahead of her. She knew that she was still young, but with all her experience, sometimes it felt like she'd lived ten lives already.

The vice president stepped forward and shook Nicky's hand. "Thank you for your service. I'm sorry for all the inconvenience."

His hand was warm and rough. His gray hair was slicked back from his forehead. Nicky felt a bit like she was being reprimanded as she shook his hand.

"Thank you, Sir," she said.

"Agent Lyons, please," he said. "I know you're only here because you're doing your job. I'm sorry for all the trouble you've had to go through."

"It's okay," Nicky assured him. "We'll do our best."

The vice president smiled. "I'm sure you will. We're going to try and make sure that no one ever threatens my daughter again. It's a shame it took a threat on her life to reform the task force, but I think it's necessary. I can't imagine what the president would do if something happened to his daughter."

"I know what you mean," Nicky said. She glanced at Natalia, then, boldly, turned to the VP.

She'd been through a lot for him, and even though he was the vice president, Nicky wanted to ask one thing of him in return.

She wanted a moment alone.

"Do you mind if we speak alone, Sir?" Nicky asked.

His eyes narrowed on Nicky, but he nodded, signaling for Natalia to wait with the two agents. Nicky and the VP stepped down the hall, just out of ear sight.

"What is it, Agent Lyons?" the VP asked. "I'll always be grateful that you saved my daughter, but—"

"I just want to know why," Nicky started, "why didn't you tell us you were going to cut off Ainsley's support?"

He took in a breath. A stern looked crossed his face, and he folded his arms. "I...I made a mistake, Agent Lyons. I've made so many mistakes. The only choice I have now is to tell my wife the truth. I know this will all come out eventually. She should know that I have another family, even if they are going to prison."

Nicky breathed deep, listening to him. "I see."

"What can I do, Agent Lyons? I have nothing to offer you or your task force. But I'm sorry for the way I treated you. I've been a terrible man. I've made terrible choices. And I realize how selfish I've been."

Nicky blinked. "It's okay. We can't all make honorable choices in our lives, Sir."

"I don't deserve forgiveness, Agent Lyons," he said. "But I'll take it, anyway."

Nicky smiled. "We're all a bit selfish every once in a while, Sir. I guess you and your family just had a bad year."

"I'm glad you understand," Cavazos said. "I would appreciate your discretion on this until I'm able to come out with it myself."

"Of course, Sir." Nicky paused for a moment, her mind going back to the woods and to the man she'd shot. Worrying so much about Ken hadn't given her much time to process the gravity of it all, and in terms of paperwork and clearing the scene, it was all still in-progress.

But Nicky had to know…

Who had she killed?

"Do we know who he was? The man who helped Marissa and James."

"Dillon Reacher," said the vice president. "Ex-military, dishonorably discharged. You'll get the official reports soon, I'm sure, but..." The vice president sighed. "Agent Lyons, you shot the man in self-defence. He was a black-market gun peddler, and he was going to kill my daughter."

Nicky nodded. "I know, Sir. It's part of the job."

Killing never felt good. Sometimes it was just necessary when it came to being a field agent. At least a man like Dillon Reacher wouldn't be around to hurt any more people. In a bizarre way, it seemed like he was almost happy to die—Nicky would never forget the strange, crazed look on his face. It disturbed her to her core.

Just as the VP was about to reply, a doctor came out of one of the rooms, holding a clipboard. "Agent Lyons?"

Nicky stepped up, hope in her heart. "Yes?"

"Agent Walker is awake now. You can go see him."

Nicky's heart leapt into her throat. She nodded once at the vice president. "Thank you, Sir. I have to go."

With that, she left, dashing after the doctor and into the room where Ken was lying on a white hospital bed.

Alive.

He was alive.

The relief was enough to drown her. Nicky rushed to the side of his bed, and his blue eyes met hers. She wanted to hug him, but she could see that he was in rough shape. He was pale and bandaged up.

But he was alive.

"Jesus, Walker," she said, catching herself. "You look like shit."

Ken laughed and shook his head. "Thanks, Lyons."

Nicky sat in the chair beside him. She found herself at a loss for words, remembering what he'd said to her before he'd lost consciousness in the woods.

He'd admitted that he had feelings for her.

Nicky's chest fluttered at the thought.

Maybe...maybe there was something between them.

She searched his face for some sort of reaction, but Ken was just looking at her, a smile across his lips.

"I'm glad you're okay," Nicky said.

"Me too," he replied. "I guess that's why you're here. You were waiting for me to wake up. If I hadn't, you'd have saved me again."

Nicky gave him a look. "I wouldn't have…"

"That's okay, Nicky," he said, smiling. "I'm glad you were here."

"Yeah," Nicky replied, marveling at the way he said her name. It was so different than when the others said it. Ken made it sound like a compliment.

Then, Ken's smile faltered. "I was worried I was going to die out there. And I was even more worried that I'd never get to tell you…"

Nicky leaned forward in her chair. She didn't dare breathe.

"You know how I feel about you, right?" Ken asked. "I know I can be kind of an asshole sometimes. But it's because I'm scared. I'm scared to lose you."

Nicky's heart swelled as her eyes stung. It didn't feel real. She had felt something growing between her and Ken for a while now, but for it to be happening—for him to feel the same was—it was surreal.

"I was terrified of losing you too," she confessed.

She lifted her hand, reaching for him. His pale skin was covered in bruises, but she didn't care. She wanted to hold him. But maybe that would be too much. Nicky settled for placing her hand on top of his.

"You're not gonna lose me," she told him. "I'm here for you, Walker. We're in this together."

Ken smiled. "No one's ever had my back like you do, Lyons. Thanks."

Nicky looked at their hands, feeling an excitement welling up in her chest. Nicky wasn't one for romance, but this was different. This was trust, building slowly but permanently between them.

"I'm sorry I didn't tell you how I felt," Ken said. "I just...I'm not good with all this. I never have been. I just wanted to tell you now, before it was too late. You were just sitting here, waiting for me, and I thought...I thought it was now or never, you know?"

There were happy tears in her eyes now. "I'm not good at this either. But I trust you with my life, Ken. I'm glad you're okay."

A smile crossed his lips, and he relaxed in the pillow. "I had Marissa…I had her right in front of me. But I was blindsided. Please tell me you got that guy…"

"I fought him in the woods," Nicky said. She let out a sigh. "I had no choice but to shoot to kill."

"Wow…" Ken looked at Nicky with empathy in his eyes. "I'm sorry. That's never easy."

"No, but at least he can't hurt anyone else."

Ken nodded. "I guess it's all okay then, huh?"

"Yes...but..." Nicky sighed. Maybe, after all this time, it would feel good to open up to someone.

Someone she trusted.

"This whole case had me thinking about my own father," she told Ken.

"Your father?" he asked, looking at her with care.

"Yeah. He's...he's a deadbeat. We don't have a relationship. Especially after my sister and I were kidnapped, and only I came back—he's blamed me for everything. But I talked to him the other day, for the first time in years, all based off something Felix Anderson said."

"Felix?" Ken lifted an eyebrow. "What did he say?"

"He thinks my dad knows something about what really happened to Rosie."

"No shit," Ken said, perplexed. "And you believe him?"

"No... I don't know." Nicky sighed. "It does feel like my whole life is going full circle. When I talked to my dad, he was as unhelpful as always. But...I wonder..."

Nicky couldn't believe that she was really thinking this, but she was.

"I think...maybe...the man who kidnapped my sister and I…"

She took a breath. Her head spun just at the idea of this, but—

"Maybe it was someone who knew my father."

CHAPTER THIRTY TWO

He made his morning coffee the same way every day: black with one cube of sugar to take the edge off. As morning light spilled through his curtains, he gazed out onto his backyard. What a beautiful day, with the sun out and shining.

Taking a sip of the bold liquid, he turned on his kitchen TV to tune into the morning news. It was always the same lately; nothing interesting enough to pull him in: break ins, petty theft, gang violence. It all bored him.

Until today.

The breaking news teaser played out above him, while the newscaster read the details: “A new ruling has been decided for kidnapper Felix Anderson, who was arrested in Florida less than two weeks ago. Anderson, who attempted the insanity plea, has been denied, and although his victims remain alive, it doesn’t look like Anderson will be leaving bars anytime soon.”

Felix...

He smiled as he sipped his coffee. Foolish little Felix. He never did have the guts...

Sitting down at his table, he opened his cell phone and looked up a name:

Agent Nicky Lyons of the FBI.

There was a photo of her on the FBI’s official website: a headshot, looking at the camera with a ghost of a smile. But he could see in her eyes that she was haunted.

Haunted by what he did.

Nicky...Those eyes...He remembered every bit of her, every exquisite beauty mark. What a wonderful person she was. Felix was lucky to have been arrested by her. She’d always been his favorite...

Why?

Don’t we always long for the one who got away?

He looked down at the screen, at the brunette woman on it, and smiled.

Maybe it wasn’t too late for them, after all.

NOW AVAILABLE!

ALL FOR ONE
(A Nicky Lyons FBI Suspense Thriller—Book 5)

When a second theater actress goes missing, FBI Special Agent Nicky Lyons, 28, must enter the world of theater to enter the killer's mind before it's too late. Was he stalking them? What drives him? And where is he hiding them?

"A masterpiece of thriller and mystery."
—Books and Movie Reviews, Roberto Mattos (re Once Gone)

ALL FOR ONE (A Nicky Lyons FBI Suspense Thriller—Book 5) is book #5 in a long-anticipated new series by #1 bestseller and USA Today bestselling author Blake Pierce, whose bestseller Once Gone (a free download) has received over 7,000 five star ratings and reviews.

Can Nicky connect the dots in time?

Or will she be doomed to play the puppet of a killer mastermind?

A page-turning and harrowing crime thriller featuring a brilliant and tortured FBI agent, the NICKY LYONS series is a riveting mystery, packed with non-stop action, suspense, twists and turns, revelations, and driven by a breakneck pace that will keep you flipping pages late into the night. Fans of Rachel Caine, Teresa Driscoll and Robert Dugoni are sure to fall in love.

Future books in the series will soon be available.

"An edge of your seat thriller in a new series that keeps you turning pages! ...So many twists, turns and red herrings… I can't wait to see what happens next."
—Reader review (Her Last Wish)

"A strong, complex story about two FBI agents trying to stop a serial killer. If you want an author to capture your attention and have you guessing, yet trying to put the pieces together, Pierce is your author!"
—Reader review (Her Last Wish)

"A typical Blake Pierce twisting, turning, roller coaster ride suspense thriller. Will have you turning the pages to the last sentence of the last chapter!!!"
—Reader review (City of Prey)

"Right from the start we have an unusual protagonist that I haven't seen done in this genre before. The action is nonstop… A very atmospheric novel that will keep you turning pages well into the wee hours."
—Reader review (City of Prey)

"Everything that I look for in a book… a great plot, interesting characters, and grabs your interest right away. The book moves along at a breakneck pace and stays that way until the end. Now on go I to book two!"
—Reader review (Girl, Alone)

"Exciting, heart pounding, edge of your seat book… a must read for mystery and suspense readers!"
—Reader review (Girl, Alone)

Blake Pierce

Blake Pierce is the USA Today bestselling author of the RILEY PAGE mystery series, which includes seventeen books. Blake Pierce is also the author of the MACKENZIE WHITE mystery series, comprising fourteen books; of the AVERY BLACK mystery series, comprising six books; of the KERI LOCKE mystery series, comprising five books; of the MAKING OF RILEY PAIGE mystery series, comprising six books; of the KATE WISE mystery series, comprising seven books; of the CHLOE FINE psychological suspense mystery, comprising six books; of the JESSIE HUNT psychological suspense thriller series, comprising twenty six books; of the AU PAIR psychological suspense thriller series, comprising three books; of the ZOE PRIME mystery series, comprising six books; of the ADELE SHARP mystery series, comprising sixteen books, of the EUROPEAN VOYAGE cozy mystery series, comprising six books; of the LAURA FROST FBI suspense thriller, comprising eleven books; of the ELLA DARK FBI suspense thriller, comprising fourteen books (and counting); of the A YEAR IN EUROPE cozy mystery series, comprising nine books, of the AVA GOLD mystery series, comprising six books; of the RACHEL GIFT mystery series, comprising ten books (and counting); of the VALERIE LAW mystery series, comprising nine books (and counting); of the PAIGE KING mystery series, comprising eight books (and counting); of the MAY MOORE mystery series, comprising eleven books (and counting); the CORA SHIELDS mystery series, comprising five books (and counting); of the NICKY LYONS mystery series, comprising seven books (and counting), of the CAMI LARK mystery series, comprising five books (and counting), of the AMBER YOUNG mystery series, comprising five books (and counting), and of the new DAISY FORTUNE mystery series, comprising five books (and counting).

An avid reader and lifelong fan of the mystery and thriller genres, Blake loves to hear from you, so please feel free to visit www.blakepierceauthor.com to learn more and stay in touch.

BOOKS BY BLAKE PIERCE

DAISY FORTUNE MYSTERY SERIES
NEED YOU (Book #1)
CLAIM YOU (Book #2)
CRAVE YOU (Book #3)
CHOOSE YOU (Book #4)
CHASE YOU (Book #5)

AMBER YOUNG MYSTERY SERIES
ABSENT PITY (Book #1)
ABSENT REMORSE (Book #2)
ABSENT FEELING (Book #3)
ABSENT MERCY (Book #4)
ABSENT REASON (Book #5)

CAMI LARK MYSTERY SERIES
JUST ME (Book #1)
JUST OUTSIDE (Book #2)
JUST RIGHT (Book #3)
JUST FORGET (Book #4)
JUST ONCE (Book #5)

NICKY LYONS MYSTERY SERIES
ALL MINE (Book #1)
ALL HIS (Book #2)
ALL HE SEES (Book #3)
ALL ALONE (Book #4)
ALL FOR ONE (Book #5)
ALL HE TAKES (Book #6)
ALL FOR ME (Book #7)

CORA SHIELDS MYSTERY SERIES
UNDONE (Book #1)
UNWANTED (Book #2)
UNHINGED (Book #3)
UNSAID (Book #4)

UNGLUED (Book #5)

MAY MOORE SUSPENSE THRILLER
NEVER RUN (Book #1)
NEVER TELL (Book #2)
NEVER LIVE (Book #3)
NEVER HIDE (Book #4)
NEVER FORGIVE (Book #5)
NEVER AGAIN (Book #6)
NEVER LOOK BACK (Book #7)
NEVER FORGET (Book #8)
NEVER LET GO (Book #9)
NEVER PRETEND (Book #10)
NEVER HESITATE (Book #11)

PAIGE KING MYSTERY SERIES
THE GIRL HE PINED (Book #1)
THE GIRL HE CHOSE (Book #2)
THE GIRL HE TOOK (Book #3)
THE GIRL HE WISHED (Book #4)
THE GIRL HE CROWNED (Book #5)
THE GIRL HE WATCHED (Book #6)
THE GIRL HE WANTED (Book #7)
THE GIRL HE CLAIMED (Book #8)

VALERIE LAW MYSTERY SERIES
NO MERCY (Book #1)
NO PITY (Book #2)
NO FEAR (Book #3)
NO SLEEP (Book #4)
NO QUARTER (Book #5)
NO CHANCE (Book #6)
NO REFUGE (Book #7)
NO GRACE (Book #8)
NO ESCAPE (Book #9)

RACHEL GIFT MYSTERY SERIES
HER LAST WISH (Book #1)
HER LAST CHANCE (Book #2)
HER LAST HOPE (Book #3)

HER LAST FEAR (Book #4)
HER LAST CHOICE (Book #5)
HER LAST BREATH (Book #6)
HER LAST MISTAKE (Book #7)
HER LAST DESIRE (Book #8)
HER LAST REGRET (Book #9)
HER LAST HOUR (Book #10)

AVA GOLD MYSTERY SERIES
CITY OF PREY (Book #1)
CITY OF FEAR (Book #2)
CITY OF BONES (Book #3)
CITY OF GHOSTS (Book #4)
CITY OF DEATH (Book #5)
CITY OF VICE (Book #6)

A YEAR IN EUROPE
A MURDER IN PARIS (Book #1)
DEATH IN FLORENCE (Book #2)
VENGEANCE IN VIENNA (Book #3)
A FATALITY IN SPAIN (Book #4)

ELLA DARK FBI SUSPENSE THRILLER
GIRL, ALONE (Book #1)
GIRL, TAKEN (Book #2)
GIRL, HUNTED (Book #3)
GIRL, SILENCED (Book #4)
GIRL, VANISHED (Book 5)
GIRL ERASED (Book #6)
GIRL, FORSAKEN (Book #7)
GIRL, TRAPPED (Book #8)
GIRL, EXPENDABLE (Book #9)
GIRL, ESCAPED (Book #10)
GIRL, HIS (Book #11)
GIRL, LURED (Book #12)
GIRL, MISSING (Book #13)
GIRL, UNKNOWN (Book #14)

LAURA FROST FBI SUSPENSE THRILLER
ALREADY GONE (Book #1)

ALREADY SEEN (Book #2)
ALREADY TRAPPED (Book #3)
ALREADY MISSING (Book #4)
ALREADY DEAD (Book #5)
ALREADY TAKEN (Book #6)
ALREADY CHOSEN (Book #7)
ALREADY LOST (Book #8)
ALREADY HIS (Book #9)
ALREADY LURED (Book #10)
ALREADY COLD (Book #11)

EUROPEAN VOYAGE COZY MYSTERY SERIES
MURDER (AND BAKLAVA) (Book #1)
DEATH (AND APPLE STRUDEL) (Book #2)
CRIME (AND LAGER) (Book #3)
MISFORTUNE (AND GOUDA) (Book #4)
CALAMITY (AND A DANISH) (Book #5)
MAYHEM (AND HERRING) (Book #6)

ADELE SHARP MYSTERY SERIES
LEFT TO DIE (Book #1)
LEFT TO RUN (Book #2)
LEFT TO HIDE (Book #3)
LEFT TO KILL (Book #4)
LEFT TO MURDER (Book #5)
LEFT TO ENVY (Book #6)
LEFT TO LAPSE (Book #7)
LEFT TO VANISH (Book #8)
LEFT TO HUNT (Book #9)
LEFT TO FEAR (Book #10)
LEFT TO PREY (Book #11)
LEFT TO LURE (Book #12)
LEFT TO CRAVE (Book #13)
LEFT TO LOATHE (Book #14)
LEFT TO HARM (Book #15)
LEFT TO RUIN (Book #16)

THE AU PAIR SERIES
ALMOST GONE (Book#1)
ALMOST LOST (Book #2)

ALMOST DEAD (Book #3)

ZOE PRIME MYSTERY SERIES
FACE OF DEATH (Book#1)
FACE OF MURDER (Book #2)
FACE OF FEAR (Book #3)
FACE OF MADNESS (Book #4)
FACE OF FURY (Book #5)
FACE OF DARKNESS (Book #6)

A JESSIE HUNT PSYCHOLOGICAL SUSPENSE SERIES
THE PERFECT WIFE (Book #1)
THE PERFECT BLOCK (Book #2)
THE PERFECT HOUSE (Book #3)
THE PERFECT SMILE (Book #4)
THE PERFECT LIE (Book #5)
THE PERFECT LOOK (Book #6)
THE PERFECT AFFAIR (Book #7)
THE PERFECT ALIBI (Book #8)
THE PERFECT NEIGHBOR (Book #9)
THE PERFECT DISGUISE (Book #10)
THE PERFECT SECRET (Book #11)
THE PERFECT FAÇADE (Book #12)
THE PERFECT IMPRESSION (Book #13)
THE PERFECT DECEIT (Book #14)
THE PERFECT MISTRESS (Book #15)
THE PERFECT IMAGE (Book #16)
THE PERFECT VEIL (Book #17)
THE PERFECT INDISCRETION (Book #18)
THE PERFECT RUMOR (Book #19)
THE PERFECT COUPLE (Book #20)
THE PERFECT MURDER (Book #21)
THE PERFECT HUSBAND (Book #22)
THE PERFECT SCANDAL (Book #23)
THE PERFECT MASK (Book #24)
THE PERFECT RUSE (Book #25)
THE PERFECT VENEER (Book #26)

CHLOE FINE PSYCHOLOGICAL SUSPENSE SERIES
NEXT DOOR (Book #1)

A NEIGHBOR'S LIE (Book #2)
CUL DE SAC (Book #3)
SILENT NEIGHBOR (Book #4)
HOMECOMING (Book #5)
TINTED WINDOWS (Book #6)

KATE WISE MYSTERY SERIES
IF SHE KNEW (Book #1)
IF SHE SAW (Book #2)
IF SHE RAN (Book #3)
IF SHE HID (Book #4)
IF SHE FLED (Book #5)
IF SHE FEARED (Book #6)
IF SHE HEARD (Book #7)

THE MAKING OF RILEY PAIGE SERIES
WATCHING (Book #1)
WAITING (Book #2)
LURING (Book #3)
TAKING (Book #4)
STALKING (Book #5)
KILLING (Book #6)

RILEY PAIGE MYSTERY SERIES
ONCE GONE (Book #1)
ONCE TAKEN (Book #2)
ONCE CRAVED (Book #3)
ONCE LURED (Book #4)
ONCE HUNTED (Book #5)
ONCE PINED (Book #6)
ONCE FORSAKEN (Book #7)
ONCE COLD (Book #8)
ONCE STALKED (Book #9)
ONCE LOST (Book #10)
ONCE BURIED (Book #11)
ONCE BOUND (Book #12)
ONCE TRAPPED (Book #13)
ONCE DORMANT (Book #14)
ONCE SHUNNED (Book #15)
ONCE MISSED (Book #16)

ONCE CHOSEN (Book #17)

MACKENZIE WHITE MYSTERY SERIES

BEFORE HE KILLS (Book #1)
BEFORE HE SEES (Book #2)
BEFORE HE COVETS (Book #3)
BEFORE HE TAKES (Book #4)
BEFORE HE NEEDS (Book #5)
BEFORE HE FEELS (Book #6)
BEFORE HE SINS (Book #7)
BEFORE HE HUNTS (Book #8)
BEFORE HE PREYS (Book #9)
BEFORE HE LONGS (Book #10)
BEFORE HE LAPSES (Book #11)
BEFORE HE ENVIES (Book #12)
BEFORE HE STALKS (Book #13)
BEFORE HE HARMS (Book #14)

AVERY BLACK MYSTERY SERIES

CAUSE TO KILL (Book #1)
CAUSE TO RUN (Book #2)
CAUSE TO HIDE (Book #3)
CAUSE TO FEAR (Book #4)
CAUSE TO SAVE (Book #5)
CAUSE TO DREAD (Book #6)

KERI LOCKE MYSTERY SERIES

A TRACE OF DEATH (Book #1)
A TRACE OF MURDER (Book #2)
A TRACE OF VICE (Book #3)
A TRACE OF CRIME (Book #4)
A TRACE OF HOPE (Book #5)

Made in United States
North Haven, CT
30 March 2023

34785292R00102